THE SEVENTH TRUMPET

BOOK ONE
THE DESERT AND THE TREE

Crystal Clark

THE SEVENTH TRUMPET
Book One: The Desert and the Tree
Copyright © 2020 by Crystal Clark

ISBN: 978-1-7334448-9-7

Library of Congress Control Number: 2020933270

Author Photo by: Mark A. France

Cover design by All Things That Matter Press

Published in 2020 by All Things That Matter Press

*To everyone who believed in me
and made this possible.*

THE FIRST TRUMPET

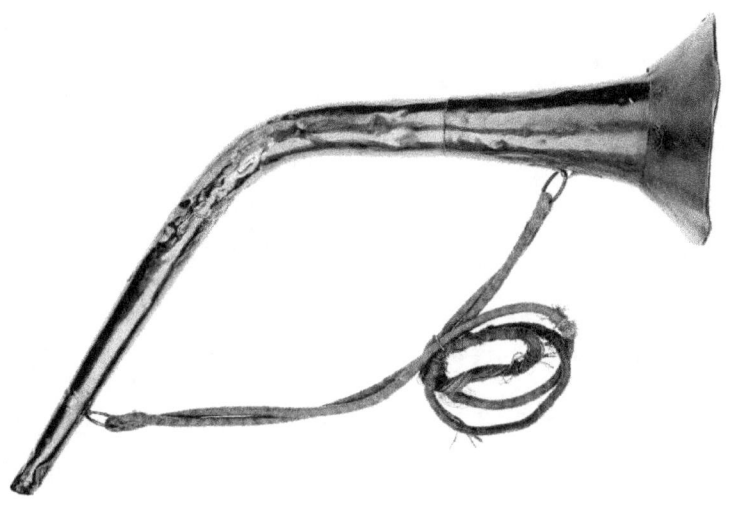

CHAPTER ONE

In last world war, the humans nearly obliterated the Earth, causing themselves to become an endangered species—as they had done to so many others before them.

I was never in favor of the humans. They have been disgusting and selfish beings ever since they were created. They have become weak and distracted. They have softened and become skipping stones against the universe. There was a time when man was the ruler over the land and the sea as well as all of the creatures that lived among them, but somehow man allowed himself to become the ruled.

Even knowing this, the Creator loves them, even now, in their end. There comes a time in every parent's life where they must accept the fate that their children have chosen for themselves. Even if it means watching them burn.

I looked around at what was left of Earth: Melahem. The aroma of burning wood and flesh was enough to make me wish that the humans had succeeded in extinguishing themselves from this land. A thick layer of smoke and smog made it difficult to see—or feel—the sun, which was probably for the best, since I was sure that their fragile skin could no longer handle direct exposure to its harsh rays.

I climbed to the top of a hill that was most likely not rock and soil but compressed garbage and ash. I looked out at the city that the humans had somehow managed to erect in the dust of a weeping parent's dreams.

I looked deep into the soul of Melahem and found nothing but darkness. So much so that I could barely feel the Light of its children. Children's souls were brighter than the rest of the humans; they were innocent. I closed my eyes and focused, attempting to find even one soul to save.

I needed to rescue the innocent before the seventh trumpet's blow. No child was ever meant to stand against the devil.

I descended the mount of lost hope and made my way towards the city. With each step, dust rose up from the dry desert-like earth that was once a beautiful forest on the edge of an ocean. With the war, most of the vegetation and wildlife was destroyed, and the water supply became scarce.

The radiation from the bombs and other weapons had created an unstable environment, most of which could not sustain any form of life. This made the crops and forests that they did manage to salvage more valuable than gold or gem stones ever were to them.

I walked through the over populated city, pushing past the masses, searching. They walked past me, through me. I was a ghost to the living; a reaper. I was not meant to be seen, except in the swift moments when I unbound a soul from its mortal body. It's mostly children and the dying who are blessed with the gift of seeing angels. Those moments in life are when the soul does the most searching and needs a strengthening of faith.

The sound of a trumpet bellowed throughout Melahem with a force so great the ground quaked. I crouched down on the trembling pebble-lined street to keep my balance.

The sound rang out like a siren, a warning. It reverberated off of the surrounding buildings for what seemed like hours, but it was truly only seconds.

"That is one," I whispered.

Screams came from my left. The force of the tremor had caused a large, unstable abandoned building to begin to crumble.

I stood up and moved closer, looking into the souls of the potential victims. There was nothing but emptiness in all of them; they were already dead.

"You wrote your own fate," I said under my breath, and I willed the building to claim its souls.

A roaring fire that only I could see sprung up around the rubble as the devil claimed seven more soldiers for his army of demons. I wished that the humans could see the hell fire; maybe then they would be more inclined to save themselves. But their fate was of their own doing.

Moments after the flames disappeared, a great roaring thunder came from the sky. Hail stones and fire came raining down over Melahem.

The few trees that lined the city caught flame; it rapidly spread throughout the dry land.

They may not be able to see Hell's fire, but at least they can see Heaven's.

I walked the streets, searching for children and the lost, anyone willing to be redeemed. I hated watching an entire planet burn in torment, even if they had brought it upon themselves.

I stood in awe of the burning city. I watched as people scrambled to save material items from the buildings. They risked their lives to collect meaningless objects that they were not going to be able to take with them in the end. I shook my head at the sight; it was pitiful. I had half a mind to finish destroying the planet myself, but I was on orders.

I've never understood the concept of possessions.

Humans have gone to war over coins, paper, and materials on countless occasions. There is no other race in the universe that places the value of life below that of a glimmering stone. The devil had impregnated this world with greed and gluttony.

I continued to the edge of the land past buildings made of stacked stones and clay. Most of them were only one story high. Their roofs were fashioned together with fallen tree branches and dried corn stalks. Although the people of Melahem were not able to farm many plants, corn has always been a resilient plant on the planet Earth. It has been around since the first days of creation and will, I imagine, be around until the end.

I looked out at the sea, Vitaquam, the polluted waters. One of the only means of food that the people of Melahem had to survive on. Their bodies had become immune to the poison that permeated the meat of every five-eyed fish and three-headed dolphin that they feasted on.

It could be assumed from their adaptation that evolution never ends. Survival is encoded into the DNA of every beast, even if they are only half alive.

I felt a tug on the sleeve of my cloak as I was staring off at the sea. A tiny dark-haired girl with olive skin and wide blue eyes was peering up at me. She could not have been any older than four years. The child's soul was the first pure thing that I had seen in Melahem. Her Light brightened everything around her. The dark waters and sand glimmered like flecks of onyx and pearl. Her presence brought beauty to the scene that mortified my being.

"You do not belong here," I said as I knelt down next to her. The little girl smiled as she reached out and touched my face. Her hand felt warm against my cheek. There was neither a drop of fear nor hate within her; she was innocent. Source of All had made children special. They understood. Born innocent, they had an innate sense of knowing. Children could see beyond the mortal world, as long as they believed.

"Are you ready to go Home?" I asked, smiling in the warmth of her light.

She nodded and wrapped her arms around my neck. "Almighty, take my sister home, set her soul free of her body so that she may leave, ashes to ashes and dust to dust." I whispered only loud enough for the two of us to hear, even if the other humans could hear me.

With my words, the child's body began to crumble in my hands. A light breeze picked up the pieces and she rose, her soul's light shining like a galaxy of stars as she floated away to freedom. I stood and watched her swirl, dancing through the clouds.

Once she was out of sight, I began to walk the shoreline. I looked down at the wet sand as I stepped. My foot did not leave an indent. There was no footprint path to be erased by the tide. I felt a sense of emptiness wash over me at the thought.

I was not sent to Melahem to interact with the humans, or even the land. I was meant to be invisible, one foot in the heavens, and one foot hovering above the earth.

"You!" a sharp voice shattered my moment of introspection.

I quickly turned to face my accuser. A tall, well-built man with hair and skin that matched the child's was storming towards me. He was dressed as a fisherman. His handwoven shirt likely was once tan but was now stained dark green from sea water. The material was cut off at the shoulders. His arms were covered in scars that told of his work at sea. The healed-over bites and cuts were reminiscent of an intricate tribal design, the mark of a warrior.

The man's face did not look like that of a warrior. It was soft, even in anger, and his eyes belonged more to a child than an grown man.

He was standing directly in front of me. Staring at me.

"How can he see me?" I whispered. I could feel his Light pulsing. It was different from the child's, but unlike an adult's. I did not recognize what he was.

"You just murdered a child," he cried.

"I just saved that child," I defended myself. The man's soul was flickering with his anger.

"From what?" he huffed, now only a few feet away from me.

"No one that innocent deserves to be around for what happens next," I said. "The hail and fire is only the beginning."

"The beginning of what?"

"The end." I paused before adding, "Are you ready to go Home?"

"What?" he shouted at me.

"I do not recognize your Light, but it is pure. You do not need to be here to watch Melahem fall," I explained.

"Watch Melahem fall?" His voice was rising in anger. "Who are you?"

He did not understand like the children and the dying. He did not have a soul that believed, yet he had a Light—and innocence.

"I will be here when you are ready," I said. I turned to continue on my way.

"Wait." I heard the man shout after me. A sensation ran though my body and I found that I could not move my legs. I pushed with all of my might, but none of my magic could break the spell that the stranger's single word had cast upon me. I was furious.

With every footstep of the man creeping up behind me, I felt my ghost-pale face redden with anger.

"What have you done to me?" I demanded. I balled up my hands into fists.

"What do you mean?" he asked innocently.

"I am immobilized," I shouted. "You commanded me to wait for you, and I waited. Why?"

"I'm sorry." He looked truly perplexed by his own power. "I didn't mean to. You can move now."

With his words, a tingling sensation ran through my legs and feet as I regained full control of my body.

"Thank you," I grumbled in an incredibly insincere manner. I was mystified. He was a human with angelic abilities. "Does that happen often, when you control people with just one word?"

"I never mean to," he said. He looked ashamed.

"Do your other family members possess this power?"

"No." He looked down at his feet. "I'm not a witch, if that's what you're wondering," he said quickly and defensively.

"I know," I reassured him as I realized what he was. He had a right to be defensive of his intentions and his character.

One of the many times that humans were given another chance to improve upon the mess that they had created, some humans were blessed and born with special abilities—what was called an Angel's Kiss—to help save the Earth from eternal damnation. It didn't happen often; perhaps it should never have happened at all. It didn't seem to have made much of a difference. In fact, it made things worse for those so gifted.

It had become human nature to hate and to fear anything that they did not understand. The Kissed humans were prosecuted. They were hunted, branded and burned as witches and demon worshipers.

Lucifer seized his opportunity in this matter and "Kissed" a select few of his own. He offered up the power of black magic. He created mass murderers, reapers of his own vision. He gave the world the dark witches that they were hunting after.

Although our plan did not work in the way we had envisioned, there were those rare few that understood their power and used it for the purpose we had intended. So we continued to Kiss a few humans in every generation up until the last war, hoping against the odds that they could save the souls of those around them.

Someone up there must have had one last hope for this planet, and he was standing right in front of me.

CHAPTER TWO

It continued to rain fire all around us as I stared at the Kissed human, perplexed, and wondering who had chosen him. He did not flinch. The apocalyptic disaster that was destroying one third of the city's vegetation, the humans' livelihood, did not seem to concern him. He was focused on me.

"So, what did you do to that little girl if you didn't kill her?" he asked in an accusing tone. "I saw her dissolve in your arms. How did that even happen?"

"She did not dissolve," I said, disgusted by the ignorance of the man's word choice. "I separated her soul from her human body. All humans begin as ash and that is what her flesh returned to."

His face twitched at my words. He began to look more and more uncomfortable by the second. The light in his soul began to flicker.

"What are you?" he asked, taking a step backwards. "Are *you* a witch?"

"No." I walked past the man and looked out at the city. The burning rain had ceased and the people were scrambling to collect any items that might be of value to them as they worked to put out the fires.

I watched as the people of Melahem dumped buckets of what I assumed was their fresh drinking and bathing water over the flames. They ran down to the sea with their empty buckets, refilled them, and ran back to their possessions.

They were more worried about putting out the fires that were consuming their belongings rather than extinguishing the flames that were destroying their trees, grasses, and crops.

"What are you?" He had positioned himself directly in my view.

"I am a reaper," I said. "An angel."

I had no reason to lie, or to not tell the human. Besides, it was a test of faith.

"I thought angels were supposed to be beautiful, and holy, and glowing." The man scoffed. He looked me up and down. I could tell that the human did not believe me. He had no reason to. In Melahem, angels were mythic creature sof lore rather than holy entities. And he was right: I did not look like any of the angels that humanity had depicted over the years. I did not fall into the human classification of beautiful. I was strong. My skin was pure white with black veins showing through. My hair was short, falling just below my ears, and was as black as my veins and the form-fitting cloak I wore. Almost my entire body was covered in tight black cloth for optimal mobility. My pupils were much more dilated than most humans were custom to seeing. To a human I looked more like their conception of a vampire than an angel, but they had never seen the demon that is a true vampire.

"I thought humans were supposed to be the image of God, but instead you have turned yourselves into his nightmare. This planet was beautiful once. It was the purest, and most intricately planned out civilization that the Maker had ever created." I looked around at the cityscape that surrounded us and shook my head in disgust.

"What is your name?" I asked.

"Lumen," he said quietly.

"Lumen," I repeated. I found humor in the irony. His name came from an ancient language and meant light, or one who will light the path. This was no coincidence; this stranger was part of The Plan.

"What is your name?" asked Lumen.

"Azrael," I said.

"Azrael. I've never heard of that name before."

"It is a name that is much older than this planet," I said, "from before humanity was even a dream." I looked deep into his glowing soul. "Are you ready to go Home?"

"Go home?" He cocked his head to the side.

"You do not have to be around to see what happens next."

"You mean that you want to do the same thing to me that you did to the little girl?" He pointed to where I had freed the child as he took a step back from me. "No."

"No?"

"I'm not going to let you kill me." He was shouting now. "I have family, people that I care about, that I need to help take care of. I need to go make sure that they are all right since *your* people sent fire down on us."

My people? So he does believe in the heavens. I did not approach Lumen but watched as his anger rose and the color of his soul changed. I had never seen anything like it before. As his emotions took over his mind, his soul went from a glowing white light to burning red. It was beautiful.

"I'm sorry," he said, breaking my concentration. He was looking around at the burning city.

"Your reaction is understandable," I told him. I followed his gaze, looking out at the city that was his home. He had every reason to be upset. Melahem was a lost city. They did not understand the rapture.

"It's all real, right?" Lumen's face was twisted in concern and his voice was shaky.

"Is what real?"

"This." He waved his hand out towards the city.

"Yes."

"I've heard stories, mostly from the older fishermen, about how Melahem was going to burn one day. They said we had to pay for our wrongdoings and for the war that created Melahem. They said the world wasn't always like this. They talk about flowers and forests, colorful animals, and cars and travel. I always thought that they were making up tales or talking about dreams that they had when they were sleeping on their boats."

"It is all true."

"So this," Lumen shoved his hands in his pockets and looked around him, "this is really the end?"

"Yes."

"We're all going to die?" Lumen's voice cracked as he spoke.

"Yes, but the innocent will be spared. They will return to the Almighty. They will go to a place where there is no pain or suffering. They do not have to watch the destruction that is to come."

"Like that little girl?"

"Exactly."

"How did you know she was innocent?"

"I could see the light in her soul," I replied. "Remember, all humans are born innocent. It is the world around them that damns them."

"Do you think that you could come out to my home? Maybe you could save my family."

"I am not here to *win* souls," I said. "I am here to *collect* souls."

"Could you just come see them? They're good people," he pleaded.

"There are many good people in the world," I said. "Just because someone is *good* does not ensure that they are innocent."

"Please." Lumen reached out and grabbed my hand. I could feel the warmth of his skin, the warmth of his light.

How can he touch me?

His hand should have passed right through me. I could touch people if I wished, but I was a ghost to their world. His Kiss was stronger than I had initially believed.

"I cannot promise where your family will go, Home or Hell," I warned.

"They will go Home," he assured me. "This way, please."

I followed in silence, scanning the land and lamenting the lack of scenery that Melahem had to offer. The people had begun to gaining control of the fires; the air was filled with thick black smoke.

As we walked through the city, I felt a strong pull towards a desert-like area a few miles beyond the edge of the city. That would be my next stop after I attended to Lumen's family.

He led me out to a line of tiny shacks standing on the middle ground between the city and the ocean. The shacks looked to be made of driftwood and speckled clay dug out of the tainted waters. Their roofs were fashioned from twine and branches of leafy trees. Some of the makeshift homes had boats parked in the front them. Men in stained clothes similar to Lumen's were repairing holes that had worn in the bottoms and sides of the boats they'd hand crafted from fallen trees and large, thick pieces of driftwood. Other men were sewing torn sails. Women were preparing and steaming fish over a fire, while children ran about, playing.

We walked for three miles before Lumen stopped in front of a tiny shack that I would not have been able to tell apart from the others if it was not for a large fruit tree in the yard. I did not recognize the fruit, but it looked to be a cross between an apple and a kiwi.

I grabbed Lumen by his arm and pulled him to the side of the house where his family would not be able to see or hear him.

"Remember, they cannot see me," I said. "Do not mention me to them and do not speak to me in front of them."

Although it would not have necessarily affected the job I'd been sent to do, there was no point in Lumen's family believing that he had gone mad.

He nodded his agreement.

Lumen pushed open a wooden door that was fastened together with a leather tie. The door was as uneven as the rest of the house looked. Everything seemed to be leaning just a little too far to the left.

There were six people inside, two men and four women. All were hard at work. The men were sanding and restringing their fishing poles, patching nets, and sharpening knives. The women were preparing fish and fruit from the tree outside. They did not seem affected by the fire that had rained down over the rest of Melahem. The heart of the city must have been the main target.

A few of the family members acknowledged Lumen's presence by looking up from their work and nodding or smiling at him, but the home remained silent and the people concentrated on their work. Lumen pulled out a filleting knife from his right pant pocket, sat down with the rest of the men, and began sharpening the tool.

I looked into each person there, but there was nothing, not even a faint flicker of hope. Their Lights had burnt out long ago, and their childhood innocence was abandoned.

They are lost. I felt a pang of sorrow for Lumen. He would have to leave his family behind now or be separated from them on the last day of the reaping—if they survived to see it.

I walked up to Lumen and brushed the side of his shoulder to get his attention. Silently, he rose and followed me back outside. No one in his family said a word in protest.

"I am sorry," I said once we'd walked around to the side of the house. "There is nothing that I can do."

"What do you mean? You can't save them?"

"No."

"Is there nothing I can do?" His voice was getting louder. I pulled him around to the back of the house where his family and neighbors would be less likely to see—or hear—him arguing with someone who wasn't their.

"You can try to help them regain their innocence, but I cannot help you with that," I told him.

"What do I do?" Tears began to well up in Lumen's eyes.

"Believe and pray." I said. "I told you, I am here to collect souls, not win them over. I could send them away from this earth now, but they would not be going Home."

"You would send them to Hell?"

"Even Hell is sweeter than the seventh trumpet's blow," I said. "I would be doing them a mercy by sending them to their eternal destiny before then."

Lumen stared at me in silence. He was breathing deeply in an attempt to calm himself. His Light was bright with anger, flickering between red and white as he fought to control his emotions.

"No." Lumen shook his head. "I'm not going to give up on them."

"That is your choice," I told him. I placed a hand on Lumen's shoulder in an attempt to comfort him in his decision before turning away walking towards the desert.

I felt sorrow for the man. He truly was filled with child-like innocence. He saw the good in everything rather than the bad, and his heart was open to believing—even in things and places that he could not see.

I understood his decision to fight for his family; he could not see the darkness that lived inside of them. Their souls were black pits, abysses of ignorance and self-pity. More people than not had fallen victim to the same fate over all of the years that Earth had supported human life. The devil had struck a strong footing with this race early in their history.

The sand of the desert was freckled with black dirt and sand that had been blown past the fisherman's town by the sea wind. I stopped walking at the sound of crunching sand echoing from behind me.

I turned to see Lumen running toward me. His feet hit the ground hard with every step. He jogged up next to me and stood at my right side.

"What are you doing here?"

"I want to stay with you," he said. "I thought that maybe if I follow you, I could learn how to save my family."

"I cannot tell you how to save your family."

"I know. But maybe I can watch you. Maybe if I can talk to you more, I will learn."

"Lumen—" I began to protest.

"Please," he begged, "I won't bother you. I know that you can't give me the answers, but maybe I can figure them out on my own if I'm around you long enough."

There was a look of determination in his eyes that told me Lumen was not going to give up hope for his family.

I had never had a companion during a reaping, and I discovered was not fond of the idea. I've always been one to keep to myself. I was meant to focus on my work. I could not stray, else I caused others to suffer.

"You can follow me through the desert and back." I sighed. "Then I am leaving you at the fishing village when we return."

"Thank you," Lumen exclaimed.

I was not thrilled about the arrangement, but I reminded myself that everything serves its purpose, and I believed this man to be a part of The Plan.

CHAPTER THREE

We walked in silence; the only sound was made by Lumen's feet crunching on the speckled sand. As we walked, Lumen never once complained about the heat, nor the distance that we were traversing. I was impressed his self-control.

I had expected a multitude of questions that I was not able to answer— did not wish to answer. It was odd having a companion walk alongside me, but it was more uncomfortably different than it was a burden.

The land was mostly flat where we were, but there were many cliffs at the edge of the desert, just before the beginning of the city. They ranged from fifty to about one hundred feet high. It gave the desert a unique look, almost like the desert was putting up a defense system against the city. Nature always has a way of working to protect itself against the terrors of humanity.

Unfortunately, the humans' wanton destruction had gone beyond what Nature could repair.

When night fell, it was nearly impossible to see the stars or the moon. The sky did nothing more than shift to a darker shade of grey than it was during the day. It seemed as though the rest of the universe had given up on Earth as well, shielding itself from the sight of a decaying humanity.

"We will stop here," I said.

"Are you sure?" Lumen asked. "We can keep going if you want to."

The human truly did not wish to be a burden on my journey.

"No." I looked up at the cloaked sky. "It is too dark now, and you are fatigued."

I had noticed that his walk had slowed. He had gone from keeping pace right at my side to walking a couple of steps behind me. I crouched down and sank my hand into the sand.

Dead. It is all dead.

I used my magic to conjure a fire. It sat smoldering on nothing but air. The use of magic sent a tingle through the tips of my fingers. It helped make me feel more connected to the planet.

I watched as Lumen sat close to the flame and rubbed his arms. I often forget how susceptible humans are to the weather. I increased the size of the flame to help him keep warm.

I sat on the ground next to him and picked up a handful of the sand with my right hand. I bit into the index finger of my left hand until the flesh broke.

"What are you doing?"

"The earth is dead," I replied.

I held my left hand over the sand and squeezed three drops of my blood onto it. We both watched as the blood spread through the sand and turned it into fertile soil. I set the soil down between us. It only took a few moments before a sprout shot up. It started out small and green, but soon grew into a fruit bearing tree that stood four feet tall.

"How did you do that?" Lumen's eyes were wide in amazement. He reached out a hand and cautiously touched the branches and leaves of the tree.

"Magic," I replied. I picked a fruit off of the tree and tossed it to Lumen.

"What is this?"

"An apple," I said. "One of the first fruits to grow from the earth. Try it."

I watched as Lumen took a small bite out of the fruit, seeming to still be unsure if it was safe to consume.

"It's sweet," Lumen said as he took a much larger bite. "Are you going to have one?"

"I do not eat," I said. "My body does not require food."

"Can you eat if you want to?"

"Only very small portions of food from Earth," I said. "Otherwise I could become ill; there are too many pollutants on this planet."

Angels used to be able to eat the fresh fruit of the earth before the industrial age began, but now, the impurities and the toxins that infested the fruits made them inedible for us.

"You hate humans," Lumen looked at me with longing eyes, "don't you?"

"Not the children," I admitted. "You should pay more attention to the children."

"The children," repeated Lumen. "Why?"

"Because you dismiss them, even though they are already everything that you are striving to become," I said. "Children are pure. They are innocent and fearless. They love and trust and have a stronger faith than most. It is the world that corrupts their fragile hearts. It is humanity that teaches them to fear and to hate. The children of your world would be better off being brought up by demons than their own kind. At least then they would be raised with strength, faith, and purpose."

"Demons," Lumen parrotted the word. His face twisted as if uttering it had left a foul taste in his mouth.

"They surround us," I said. "Demons *are* real."

"That's why you want to save the innocent? Because of the demons?"

"Yes. They do not deserve to be around when the devil is allowed to have his turn with the people of Earth."

"What is going to happen?"

I closed my eyes and took a deep breath as I thought of the terrors that were to come in Melahem's future. Earth had been a toy for Lucifer. He played with it like a child burning ants with a magnifying glass. He enjoyed torturing the humans; he relished watching them squirm. I was not ready to see what he had in store for the planet once he was allowed to have full reign.

"The barriers that hold back the devil and his army will be dropped," I said. The words made my stomach turn over.

"His army?"

I nodded.

"Demons." Lumen's voice cracked.

"Yes."

"So we are all going to die," said Lumen. His face dropped as he spoke the words. The thought of death always brought a feeling of sorrow to the humans.

"Yes," I affirmed his statement, "but that was never a question. The only way off of the Earth is through death."

"Why? Why is there a dark end to everything?"

"Death is not a dark end," I said. I found myself feeling irritated by his statement.

"How is it not?"

"Humans." I shook my head. "You waste your life fearing and evading death instead of embracing it. You see beauty in the death of leaves, in the rebirth of plants in the spring, but not in the death and rebirth of your own kind. It saddens you. You mourn and weep and wallow when you should be celebrating the freedom that person has just received."

Lumen sat in silence. He looked as though he was truly thinking about what I had said to him. Most of the humans left in Melahem had no idea what the true meaning of death was.

"What was Melahem like before it was … this?" asked Lumen, changing the subject.

"Earth," I said, "was perfect."

I waved my hand over a small area of the desert floor and pulled a small amount of energy from the soil that I had created. I projected pictures, small glimpses of my memory into the sand for Lumen to see.

"The oceans were filled with the water." I narrated the visions. "Its waves danced in the sunlight. The land was full of trees and shrubs and grasses. There were more species of animals than you could count. They filled the land, the sea, and the air. Some of the creatures were so beautiful that even I thought that Creator had plucked them straight out of Heaven and placed them on Earth."

"What happened to them?"

"Humans," I said plainly. I pulled my hand back up to my knee and the memories disappeared from the ground. I could feel my anger towards the humans rise as I remembered everything that they had ruined. "Humans were created, and they destroyed everything. They became filled with greed, hate, and fear. They allowed evil to rule their minds. They lost their innocence."

"Not every human is terrible," asserted Lumen. He looked down at his feet and then at me.

"No, not *every* human," I agreed. I could not help but stare at my companion. He did not argue with what I said, he did not challenge me; he only believed.

There was a soft distant sound of sand shifting under pressure. Then something else, like a muffled voice.

"Did you hear that?" I asked Lumen.

"Hear wh—"

"Shh!" I cut him off before he could finish answering my question. I heard it again: a low growl. I could not place where is was coming from; it seemed to be all around us.

I sat straight up and surveyed the land that surrounded us. I could not see anything. I raised my right hand up into the air and conjured a flame to hover above us. The light reflected off multiple sets of eyes that I did not recognize.

We were surrounded.

"What is that?" asked Lumen. "Is that a demon?"

"That creature is neither of Heaven nor Hell," I said. "You humans created that beast."

The creatures walked on all fours and had the deep, low growl of a wolf. Their eyes were red like sin and half of the flesh on their bodies looked to be either missing or burnt. Faces were covered in blackened crisp flesh. The bones of the monsters' shoulder blades broke through their backs like wings.

They were creeping closer to us, slowly stalking, in pack formation.

"Do not move," I warned Lumen.

I stood up slowly and counted; there were six of them. I extinguished the flame in my hand, and stepped out towards the creatures, away from Lumen. Three of them began to watch me, while the others kept their gazes on Lumen.

They can see me. Interesting.

I moved in front of Lumen; it would be safer to keep the pack together. I put my hand to the ground and set an electric shock through the sand. I made it strong enough to scare, but not injure the creatures. I refused to kill any animal that was doing nothing more than following its own instincts.

The shock did not affect them. The beasts stopped for only a moment before continuing to stalk the human and me. They were coming faster now.

Lumen stood up behind me. He reached down and picked up a large stone and pulled back his arm to throw it at the beasts. I put up my hand to block his throw.

"That is not necessary," I said, taking the rock from his hand.

I put my hand to the ground again. This time, I reached deeper into the earth until I could feel energy, life. I arched the energy into a shield, lifted it, and planted the energy firmly around us. I had to pull more energy from the ground as, in physical form, my own being did not contain enough power to complete such a large task on its own. The art of Energy Siphoning was only taught to a few select angels and Kissed beings who Creator believed could be trusted with the knowledge. Unfortunately, before his fall from our Maker's court, my brother was also taught the skill—and excelled at it.

The power glowed deep purple and red. It was beautiful, like a moonrise on Corton. The Cortonions saw beauty in darkness and shadows. They believed that the light blinds one from the truth, but that in the darkness one sees who they really are.

I always found that philosophy to be true. On all of the planets that I had reaped and watched, one observation stood true for all of them. It is in the darkest times that one has to fight the hardest. They have to fight because it is the struggle that makes them strong. When raised in the light, they forget about—or fear—the dark. When it is necessary to fight for light, for hope, it causes them to truly appreciate the light but respect the darkness. So many forget to respect the darkness.

The glowing shield stood strong in front of us. There was enough energy deep in the earth to keep us safe for the night. I reached up to the top of the shield and pulled the energy down around us, creating a dome.

I sat down next to the fire and watched as the creatures circled us in confusion. They took turns lunging at the shield, becoming more aggressive and frustrated each time they bounced back with a shock.

"Are we just going to leave those things out there?" Lumen asked. His voice was trembling.

"Yes." I did not look away from the animals as they began to walk away. "We are safe in here."

"Shouldn't we kill them?" Lumen was almost shouting. "What if they come back?"

"You do not need to kill them; you need to understand them," I said with annoyance. "As soon as the human race learned to fear, they began to kill everything that they did not understand. They ruined and lost so much … so much beauty, so much hope and freedom. Now this is all that is left."

I picked up a handful of sand and watched as it fell between my fingers.

"What is this?" Lumen reached out to touch the dome.

I jumped and pulled his hand away before the wall electrocuted him.

"Energy," I replied. "I pulled it from the living earth beneath the sand and ash."

"How?"

"Magic."

"What is your magic? Where does it come from? You can make fire, and soil, and plants grow, and this." He gestured toward the energy dome. "How?"

"Everything is connected," I began. "The plants, the water, the heavens, and Hell. Everything is connected to Source of All, because It created everything. There is an energy that runs through you, just as there is an energy that runs through me."

I grabbed Lumen's hand and shoved it deep into the earth. I pulled energy from the ground while I held his hand so that he could feel the strength of the connection that he had with everything that surrounded us.

"Can you feel that?"

"I feel like my arm is going numb," he said. "It tingles and burns, but it doesn't hurt."

"Close your eyes," I instructed him, "and concentrate on those beasts that were surrounding us. Picture their faces."

Lumen's eyes were closed tight.

"Can you see them?"

"Yeah."

"Good," I said. "Choose one. Concentrate on it. See the world through its eyes. Smell what it smells, feel what it feels."

I pulled more energy from the ground and pushed it through Lumen's fingertips to help him feel the energy of the animal pulsing through him.

I watched as his face twitched. His nose wrinkled up and he sniffed the air. I could see his eyes moving back and forth behind his eyelids. His body spasmed, and I could tell he was inside the mind of the beast.

After a few moments, I pulled his hand from the earth and released my grip on him.

Lumen shook his head and rubbed his hands over his eyes as though waking from a deep sleep. He looked down at his hands and examined them. He touched the tips of his fingers together, and a few lingering sparks of energy shot through the air.

"What did you see?" I asked.

"The pack," he replied. "I was walking in the back of the pack. I could feel the sand between my paw pads. I could see everything in the desert. My vision was only red and grey. There were no colors. I could smell … us, and I was hungry for flesh, any flesh. The pack needs to eat."

"You could feel them," I said.

"Yes," Lumen said. Sorrow washed over his face. "They are all so hungry. They're just hunting to survive."

"I have watched them hunt before. They are forced to live in the shadows of the city where they have their caves to shield them from what is left of the sun. The rays of the sun burn their skin, and if they travel too far away from their caves, the injuries to their bodies are too severe, and they do not make it home. We just happened to wander into their territory. Do you see now why I would not allow you to harm the beasts?"

"Yes. I'm sorry. I didn't think about why they were hunting us, I was just—"

"Afraid," I finished his sentence.

Lumen nodded. He looked ashamed.

"That is human nature," I said. "Fear is what drives you, as well as what destroys you. You need to learn to control it."

"How?"

"Practice, patience, and faith."

Lumen sat in silence. What he had seen was a lot for anyone to process, especially a human.

"You should rest." I motioned for Lumen to lie down. "Tomorrow will not be easy."

Lumen nodded in agreement and lay his head next to the fire. I sat up and watched the light from the dome swirl around us, purple and white, like fairies dancing with lightning bolts.

CHAPTER FOUR

Morning came early for us, as we still had a long way to walk before we reached the souls I was being drawn to. I shook Lumen awake just before dawn. There was a light haze to the sky as the morning sun attempted to break through the darkness of the night.

I lowered the energy dome that I had conjured to keep out the wolf-like beasts that we had encountered during the night. As Lumen began to stir, I put out the flame that was keeping him warm against the cold desert sand. I watched as he stretched and forced himself awake.

I looked out at the desert and mapped out the path that we would follow for the day. A fog had blanketed the desert floor during the night and made it difficult to see farther than a few feet past our campsite.

I reached my hand into the earth and summoned an apple tree as I had done when we had first stopped for the night.

"Eat," I instructed Lumen. "We have a long walk ahead of us today."

Lumen nodded and plucked the fruit from the tree. I walked the perimeter of our campsite while he ate. There was no sign of the animal pack. Indeed, there was no sign of any form of life. I stood and listened for anything that might have been lurking in the fog. The world was silent. The only sound in the desert was the echo of Lumen biting into his apple.

"Are you ready?" I asked when I returned to his side.

He nodded as he plucked the last apple from the tree and dropped it into his pocket. When he stood up, the tree descended back into the ground.

Lumen walked at my right side as we left the campsite behind us. There was a chill to the morning air; I breathed in deep and felt refreshed as the cold air filled my lungs.

I had always enjoyed the brisk air of the morning and missed the days when morning dew coated lush grasses. I would sit and watch as it sparkled in the sunlight, reflecting the vibrant colors of the forest flowers.

As we walked, the fog began to lift, and the sun worked its way up into the sky. The heat began to beat down on us and Lumen's pace started to slow.

"Let us rest for a couple of minutes," I said. "You need water."

Lumen did not protest my suggestion to rest this time. He sat down on the hot desert sand and pulled the remaining apple from his pocket.

As he ate, I conjured a freshwater spring from the sandy ground. Water shot up like a fountain, two feet into the air.

I cupped my hands to catch the water and brought it my mouth. Sweet and pure, it tasted as water had when Earth was first born. It was untainted from the pollution of cities.

Lumen knelt down beside me and drank deeply.

"This water is delicious," he stated.

"It is pure," I replied. "This is how water tasted before the wars."

Lumen stuck his head into the flow of the water and let it run over him. He rubbed the water over his face and the back of his neck to cool himself.

"Thank you," he said as he rose from the water spring.

"Of course." I nodded. "Are you ready to finish our journey? We are not far now."

"I'm ready," Lumen confirmed.

I could feel the strength of the souls growing as we continued on our way through the desert.

After we'd trekked another five miles, I could see a break in the horizon. There was a large fence, and what looked like the top of a house.

"We are close," I said to Lumen. "Can you see the house in the distance?"

He nodded.

The air seemed easier to breathe the closer we got to the home. It was difficult to see the house against the desert sand as it was only a few shades lighter than the surrounding ground. It was built of a combination of twigs, sand, bone, and stones; a home erected in the middle of a wasteland.

As we got closer, I could tell that they'd used whale bones as the skeletal structure of the walls. Before the war, the Atlantic Ocean used to reach far beyond the desert, but when the ocean receded to become the sea that the people of Melahem fished, many creatures did not follow the waves. Whales, sharks, and other large sea dwellers were trapped, became beached, and left only the sand and bones of the magnificent creatures that used to roam free in what once was one of the largest bodies of water in existence.

There were more bones, tied together with rope, creating a fence around the dwelling. The ribs were curved out towards the desert and the tips of the bones were carved into sharp points, making them look more like teeth than the ribs of a large mammal. I assumed that was to help keep out the creatures that we had encountered during the night, or others that we had not yet come across.

I unlatched a rope that held shut a stiff gate of bone. I had to push harder than I had expected to open it. It was clear that the gate had not been opened in a long time. Sand had blown up against it, reinforcing the fence. As I pushed the gate open, sand rolled off of the fence and began filling in the groove left by the gate.

Once Lumen and I could both fit through the gap. I stopped pushing. I did not force the gate shut behind us. The people who lived there would no longer require its protection.

As we walked towards the house, I could see the years of care and experienced craftsmanship that had gone into building it. The structure was beautifully constructed, especially given the materials that the builder had to work with. The closer that we got, the more detailed the pile of sticks and bones became.

There were etchings in the outer bone layer of the walls: dates, times, and a variety of symbols. The bone and wood that arched into a doorway had been carved to look like the branches of a blooming tree. Colorful pebbles and stones were carefully placed to create a patio that was graced with handcrafted furniture. A large bench rested against the back of the building and around a stone fire pit with a flame flickering inside sat two rocking chairs.

As we stepped onto the patio, an elderly man walked through the doorway. He was dressed in simple clothes: a brown long-sleeved shirt and tan pants that matched the dessert. He was carrying a dead rabbit by its back legs in one hand and a bone blade in the other. He looked directly at me as he sat down on the bench.

"It's about time," he said. He slid the blade between the rabbit's fur and flesh and began to skin the creature.

"You know who I am?" I asked.

"My wife and I have been praying for you to come by for years," he said.

His face was worn, his skin darker than the people in the city. There were less toxins in the desert, so he was exposed to more sunlight. His long gray beard was braided down to his chest. His scarred hands showed his age.

"Are you ready then?"

"After dinner," he said, the lilt in his voice making his words an almost-question. "Viola's always dreamed about dining with the angels."

I smiled my agreement.

He motioned to the rocking chairs next to the fire pit. Lumen, wide-eyed, appeared both amazed and perplexed at our situation.

I gestured towards the chairs and he followed me past the man, not sitting until I did.

"Who do I have the honor of being in the presence of?" asked the man, looking up from his work. His voice was rough, but his eyes, a mix of shades of blues and grays, were soft, like the calm after a storm.

"I am Azrael," I introduced myself. "And this is Lumen."

"I'm not an angel, though," Lumen spat out the words.

"Mmm-hmm," grumbled the man. "Not like her, at least."

I could feel Lumen looking at me, and suspected he was hoping for explanation. I was not sure if I had one to give him, so I kept my focus on our host.

"I'd introduce myself, but I'm gonna guess that you already know since you're here and all," he said.

"Caleb and Viola Waters," I acknowledged.

Of all of the souls that I had come here to save, they were the only two I knew by name. I had been watching over and listening to them for years. They had prayed for me to come, for the world to be put out of its misery. They had known all along that the end of Melahem would be coming within their lifetime. They had tried to save a few others from the evil that they believed had consumed the city. No one ever believed them enough to follow them, so they lived in the desert alone.

They left the city when the pollution had taken their first and only child. The baby could not breathe in the smog. She was only three weeks old.

"How are you surviving out here, so far away from the city water?' asked Lumen.

"How are you surviving drinking the city water?" countered Caleb. He motioned to the back of the house, pointing his thumb behind him. "I struck a freshwater well when Viola and I first came out here. That's why we built our home here."

"A well?" asked Lumen. "It hasn't dried up?"

"Hasn't yet. That's what faith'll get you."

Caleb reached under the bench and pulled out a large bone skewer and pushed it with ease through the rabbit carcass.

"Excuse me," Caleb said, rising to his feet. "I need to rub it down with salt."

When Caleb was out of our vision, Lumen looked at me, his mouth hanging open, lost for words, not sure what question he should ask me first.

"How have they been surviving out here for so long?" Lumen finally settled on a beginning. "Alone?"

"Caleb told you," I replied. "Faith."

Lumen did not look satisfied with my answer.

"There is a significantly lower percentage of pollution out here in the desert than there is in Melahem," I added.

"I'm having a difficult time breathing out here, though I can breathe

26

without any issues in the city," said Lumen.

"That is because you are used to the thick, smog-filled air. You have grown a tolerance for it. The air is thinner and cleaner out here."

There was a rustling noise from the kitchen, followed by the sound of plates clinking together, then footsteps sounding ever closer.

When Caleb returned, there was a glowing woman at his side. She was painfully thin, with long silver hair flowing down to the middle of her back, and soft blue eyes that matched her husband's. I watched as a tear rolled down her cheek and she brought her hands up to her face.

"Of all of the stars to fall from the sky, one finally landed at my back door," she said. "It is an honor."

She walked up to me and stroked my cheek with a trembling hand. I stood, taking her hands in mine.

"*Puer dei*," I said. "The honor is mine." I kissed her forehead and drew an invisible cross with my thumb where my lips had met her skin. This was the customary whenever an angel and an elder soul met for the first time. Her heart was more pure and full of light than any other that I had seen, which was why I had been watching Caleb and Viola for so long. She truly enchanted me.

She sat on the bench next to her husband as he began to roast the rabbit. They spoke with us about their life in the city and how it had taken their baby girl from them. I listened to the story that I had been watching unfold over the last fifty years.

"We were just children when I met Caleb," Viola reminisced. "Even at a young age, we knew that we wanted to get out of the city.

"I came from a family of fishermen. People thought it was normal to catch a fish with three heads and eyes growing straight down its back, but I always knew that something was wrong, something unnatural about the creatures we pulled from the water. There was something abnormal about the whole city.

"I was thirteen years old when I met Caleb. He was the only person who believed me when I told them that I felt wrong about living in Melahem.

"As we grew and our relationship strengthened, we promised each other that we would leave the city. We tried to talk our families into leaving with us, but they refused. It was hard to accept that our families would no longer be a part of our lives."

I watched as tears began to roll down Viola's face. Her eyes were unfocused, dreamy, as she looked into the past and watched her life replay before her eyes.

"Then I got pregnant," she said. Her face fell as sorrow washed over her. "We decided to stay in the city until the baby was born so that our parents could at least meet their new grandchild before we moved. She only lived a few weeks. The poor angel couldn't breathe. The smog filled her lungs and stole her from us before we could get her out of the city.

"Faith. That was her name, my daughter." Viola's voice cracked.

"It's an awful feeling, burning the body of an infant, your three-week-old child. It seems like it should be a sin," said Caleb.

He grabbed his wife's hand with the hand he was not using to turn the spit holding the rabbit.

"We made it out of the city the next morning," Caleb continued. "It wasn't easy adjusting to our life out here, but we knew it was the right decision for the both of us.

"The creatures out here are a lot different from anything you'd encounter in the city. The world is untamed and free. All the new animals we encountered kept us moving, searching for water and a safe place to build a shelter. We were thinking of giving up and turning back to the city when we finally struck our freshwater well in the back there." Caleb motioned to the back of the house with his head.

"We were lucky to find enough old bones to build a solid fence. I put in a gate, but once the fence was complete, we never once opened it. Never needed to."

I watched as Lumen listened in awe. It was rare for any human to live past forty in Melahem. Between the pollutants, the radiation, and the lack of an ozone layer, any life at all was truly a miracle.

When the rabbit was done, Caleb pulled it from the flame. Its blackened, crackling flesh reminded me of the creatures that had stalked us in the desert the night before.

"Please, come inside." Viola led us into their home.

Once seated around the table, I accepted the plate of meat, raw vegetables, and fruit that I was offered. Lumen gave me an odd look for accepting the meal, but did not say a word.

"I always dreamed of having dinner with the angels." Viola smiled at Lumen and I as she bit into a carrot.

"Now you will live your dream every night of your eternal life," I said.

I made sure to sample all of the foods I was offered, because I did not want to offend the couple. The food was some of the best that I had ever tasted on Earth. Nothing could compare to the taste of the sweet fruits from before humanity gave in to temptation, but this was close.

I ate all that my body could tolerate. Even though the food was purer than anything in the city, it was still plagued with radiation and toxins.

"What does Heaven look like?" asked Viola. "I've dreamed of it looking so many different and beautiful ways, I can't decide how I hope it will actually look."

"Well," I began, "there have been many tales that humans have made up about Heaven over the years, and most of them are very false. I do not believe that the humans' depiction of Heaven does it justice whatsoever. When you first arrive, are not met at a large silver gate perched upon clouds. There is no entrance. It is a vast abyss of glory that is specific to each person who is lucky enough to arrive there. Your Heaven depends on you. You may arrive on a path in the middle of a lush forest surrounded by animals and drenched in sunshine. You may be sitting on a white sand beach watching dolphins play on diamond encrusted wave. You may be floating among the stars, admiring the beauty of the universe.

"Wherever you are, though, the Creator will come to you. You will lay eyes on the form you choose the Maker to appear in, and all of the questions you have about life, death, and the universe will be answered. You will be filled with knowledge and peace."

"Will Caleb and I be together?" asked Viola.

"If you wish," I replied. "You may see anyone you wish who resides there. Everyone is connected. If you wish to see someone in particular, all you have to do is think it, and it will be done."

I watched as a smile spread across Viola's face. She reached across the table and squeezed her husband's hand.

I could see Lumen leaning over the table towards me. He seemed to be amazed at the truths that I was speaking about.

"It would be possible to be with your entire family, if they were all allowed in?" asked Lumen,

"It would." I said.

Lumen nodded at my affirmation of his thought. He was still hopeful that he was going to be able to save his family. He did not understand how difficult it is to bring light to a soul that has been dark for many years.

"Thank you for the delicious meal," I thanked Viola and Caleb.

"The honor is ours," said Caleb. "I apologize that we did not have more to offer."

"It was not necessary for you to offer anything. You have been more than gracious," I said.

I helped Viola clear the table and saw her eyeing the pile of dirty dishes.

"No need to worry yourself with those," I said.

"No," she agreed. "I suppose not."

I took her hand and led her into the sitting room to her husband. They sat on a couch that Caleb had crafted out of driftwood. The detail that he had put into the piece was magnificent. He truly was blessed with talent.

"Thank you for inviting us into your home," I said. "The meal was as delightful as the company."

"Thank you." Viola blushed.

"Are you ready?"

"We've been waiting a long time for this," said Caleb. He grabbed his wife's hand and nodded to me as they laced their fingers together.

I placed a hand on each of their shoulders and closed my eyes.

"Maker, take my brother and sister home. Set their souls free of their bodies so that they may leave. Ashes to ashes, and dust to dust."

As soon as I uttered the last word, their bodies began to crumble. A light breeze came through a window in the sitting room and carried their sparkling ashes out and up to the heavens.

I turned to see Lumen staring out the window with tears cascading down his cheeks. I stood next to him, watching as the last few glistening ashes disappeared into the sky. The sun was beginning to set. We were far enough away from the city that we could see colors in the sunset. Instead of a light grey sky fading into the night, the sky was painted with pinks and oranges and different shades of purple.

We sat on the porch and watched as the colors shifted into the deep blues of twilight. I sparked a fire in the stone pit that Caleb had used to cook the rabbit. The heat felt nice as the night air began to cool.

"We have another long walk back to the city tomorrow," I reminded Lumen.

"Can you see any souls from here?"

"No," I replied. "The Waters' had the brightest souls of anyone in Melahem. I cannot feel the light of anyone in the city from here."

"You will when we get closer, though?"

"I hope so."

I looked up at the night sky and I could see the stars. They were faint, but they were still up there. Being on Melahem, even for only a couple of days, had made me forget about the beauty of the universe that surrounded the dying planet. I wished that there was still some hope for Earth.

We retired for the night. I helped Lumen gather blankets and pillows to form a makeshift bed on the floor of the sitting room. Neither one of us felt comfortable lying in the bed of the deceased. Once Lumen was settled, I made my way to the front of the house.

I sat in the doorway and allowed the cool night breeze to fill the house. The air was relaxing and appreciated after the long, hot walk through the desert.

In the distance, I heard a creature howl. Soon after, many more howled in return. I imagined they were the same beasts that Lumen and I had encountered. Then there was another sound, deeper than the howls. It was a low-pitched growl that I did not recognize.

The howling stopped, and the sound of padded paws hitting the ground took its place. Something had frightened, and, I assumed, wa, chasing the beasts.

I looked back into the house at Lumen. I could hear him breathing lightly; he was sound asleep. I turned back to the night, keeping my eye on the fence that I had left open when Lumen and I had first reached the house.

The thought of leaving Lumen alone in the house long enough to close the gate made me uneasy. Plus I knew that any magic would most likely wake him, so I settled for keeping watch through the night.

CHAPTER FIVE

We rose with the dawn; it was a long walk back to Melahem. I was sad to leave the home in the desert. It was refreshing to be able to breathe such clean air and to be able to see the stars at night. I needed to move on, though. I was charged with searching the city for the innocent, even if there were only a few — or even one — left.

"It's all dead," I heard Lumen mutter, "and the well is dry."

"It was only here for them," I said, gesturing at the wilted orange tree. "Their faith made the food and water possible, and now that they are gone, it has all passed with them."

I pushed my hand down into the pot of the orange tree and pulled the last bit of energy from its roots. There was just enough left for one orange to form on a sagging branch. I plucked the fruit and handed it to Lumen.

"It is amazing what faith can do," I said.

"It is," Lumen agreed as he accepted the orange. Juice ran down his hands as he peeled the fruit. A smile cracked across his face as he tasted its sweet meat.

Once Lumen was fed and ready, we began our journey back to the city. When we reached the whale bone gate, I looked back at the Waters' house. It truly was a beautiful structure. I squeezed through the gate behind Lumen and we began our trek through the desert, away from the little utopia.

I searched as far as I could see in every direction, looking for any sign of the creatures I had heard during the night. Although I possessed no fear of any animal, I did hope for our journey back to Melahem to be a smooth one. I assumed that, as we saw nothing during the day, that the beasts only came out after the sun fell.

We passed the spot where we had stopped for the night on our way into the desert. The sun was high and the air began to thicken with pollution the closer that we got to the city.

As we walked, the sky turned overcast and thunder rumbled overhead. A breeze picked up and carried with it the sweet smells of vanilla and cherry blossoms. My mind raced.

He should not be here. I could feel my anger stirring within the pit of my stomach.

"What is that smell?" asked Lumen. He breathed deeply of the intoxicating aroma.

"My brother," I growled. It was not time for his arrival. Only the first trumpet had sounded. I still had time.

"Your brother?"

As he spoke, the sky above us darkened to such a degree that I could not see even three inches in front of myself. I conjured a flame and looked around, at the same time reaching out my free hand and grabbing Lumen by the arm. I was not sure what sort of trick my brother was attempting to pull, but he was not going to snatch Lumen from my side.

He appeared from the shadows wearing a simple black suit that matched his eyes and veins. He looked poised and relaxed, as always, as he sauntered towards us, hands in pockets, lips curled in the slightest show of a smile. A bolt of lightning cracked across the dark sky, momentarily blinding me. When my vision had refocused, my brother was gone.

"Hello, sister," I heard him sneer.

I turned to see him standing behind us. A loud crack of thunder rumbled above us. My brother had always enjoyed theatrics. I pulled Lumen closer to my side as my brother walked up to him. Lumen's mouth opened, but he was lost for words as my brother began to caress Lumen's face with the back of his hand. My brother's smile had grown; his coal black lips were pulled thin with joy. He walked behind Lumen. He licked the base of Lumen's neck, up to his ear, and smiled at me.

"You taste better than I expected," he hissed in Lumen's ear. "Sinful. Nice choice, sister."

"Lucifer," I snapped.

Lucifer smiled broadly, showing off his perfectly white fangs. "Come, sister," his voice took a more serious tone, "we have business to discuss."

I stood, frozen and furious, going over every reason that I could think of for my brother's premature arrival. He had never interfered with a reaping before. His time was after the seventh trumpet's bellow. Then, and only then, could he wreak whatever havoc and terror on the humans he wished. Until then, the planet was mine.

"Do not worry." He smiled at Lumen. "We will just be up there."

He pointed to a cliff that I did not remember seeing the first time Lumen and I had walked through the desert. The idea of Lucifer creating a cliff for dramatic effect was not surprising to me.

"You will be able to keep an eye on your pet from up there," he said to me.

"Stay here," I commanded my companion, whose face showed his fear.

Lumen nodded, keeping his eyes fixed on Lucifer.

Before I could say a word in protest, Lucifer came up behind me and placed his hand on my shoulder to teleport us to the top of the cliff, about two hundred feet above the desert floor. We were high enough to see the entire cityscape of Melahem, but also close enough that I could look down on Lumen and see that he was not harmed.

"Disgusting, is it not?" asked Lucifer. He stood next to me so that we were observing the same view of the city.

"What are you doing here?" I snapped.

"I am here to make you an offer, sister."

"No." I said sharply. I had heard my brother's "offers" before, and they all ended in more bloodshed than necessary. I had seen him make deals with other angels and powerful beings, and they all ended in his favor, with whomever he made the deal with ultimately forced into his army.

"I think that you will like this one," he said. "I am willing to trade you the souls of all of the children that would belong to me after the seventh trumpet … for your pet." He waved down at Lumen. "I do know how much you love the children."

"Their souls are not for barter."

"Are you so sure about that?"

He relished seeing himself as a higher being. Humans, and other people that had been created, were just playthings to Lucifer. He enjoyed nothing more than pulling their strings and watching them dance—especially if he could make an angel dance along with them.

"Their fate is their own," I said, pointing down at Melahem. "I am here to reap, not to interfere."

"And just what exactly are you doing with that one?" he asked, motioning to Lumen.

It made me uneasy to look in Lumen's direction; my brother and I had moved just far enough to the other side of the cliff that I could no longer see Lumen from where I was standing.

"His light is already pure," I said. "I do not understand why you believe that he can be yours to claim."

I took a step sideways to the left so that I could see Lumen. Lucifer followed my movement and blocked my view so that I could only see him.

"Lights flicker, sister, and, with some, a light breeze is enough to snuff them out."

"Not this one," I argued.

"Hmm." Lucifer ran his fingers through his thick black hair. "We will see."

He locked his right elbow around my left and twirled me around, back towards the city. We stood in silence gazing over Melahem. It was a disgusting sight. I mulled over Lucifer's words. Why was he so interested in Lumen? Was it because he was marked with an angel's Kiss? He has Kissed many of his own who were much stronger than Lumen. And why was he willing to offer me all the lost children? They were his favorite to claim; he loved watching my heart break as the flames of his Hell consumed them.

I turned my head at the sound of sand crunching behind us. Lumen was making his way towards us. I now realized why Lucifer had been distracting me from the side of the cliff that Lumen was standing under.

"What are you doing?" I said. "I told you not to come up here."

"Did you come up here to meet your fate face-to-face?" Lucifer dropped my arm and reached out a hand to Lumen.

I slapped his hand away with a quick spark. "What do you think you are doing?" I could feel my anger rising.

"Just claiming what is soon to be mine, sister," he sneered.

"Not this one." I wedged myself between the two of them. "He is mine."

"But his soul—"

"Is pure," I cut him off. "He is innocent."

He slithered up close so that his face was almost touching mine. "What is your definition of innocent?" he murmured. "We will see how long you both last. I *want* this one."

He stepped back and took a long look at Lumen.

"Until then, sister. My offer stands." He bowed and vanished into a sparkling cloud of smoke.

The sky cleared and I could see that the sun was almost halfway down now. Lumen and I were back on the desert floor; the cliff had disappeared with my brother.

"Your brother is the devil?" Lumen shouted.

"Even the devil was once an angel," I said, still watching the smoke dissipate.

"Did you know he was going to try to take me with him?"

"No."

"Why would he want me?"

"Because of your soul."

"My soul?" He looked dumbfounded.

"It is not fully human," I explained. "You have an angelic hue, a glimmer. It is why you can see me. He sees winning you over as a challenge, a victory."

"So I'm an angel?" His face brightened as he spoke the words.

"No," I said, and his face fell with disappointment. "But you have been blessed. It is where you get your power. It is called the Angel's Kiss. Some humans are given a gift of natural power to help them to connect with the Earth."

"Witches?"

"Witches, seers, wiccans, they have been called by many names." I said. "The ones who have been blessed by us were given their powers in an attempt to save the Earth—and humanity—but they became hated and feared for their powers. They were hunted and burned.

"Then there are others who have been touched by my brother," I continued. "He introduced the world to black magic and sorcery. His people conjure demons and raise the dead, playing the hand of God and causing an unbalance in the universe."

Lumen stared blankly at me as he attempted to process what I was saying.

"It was the lack of stability and faith in the world that caused Earth to be dissolved into Melahem," I said.

"So this is your brother's fault?" Lumen asked. "The world is ending because of him?"

"My brother played a hand in this, but so did we. Each human has written their own fate."

"Why didn't you tell me what I was?" Lumen ran his fingers through his hair and turned away from me while emitting a scream.

"Because you would not understand," I said.

"Because I wouldn't understand?" He was shouting again. "I haven't understood what was wrong with me and why I'm different from everyone else my entire life! I've been pretending to be normal for the last twenty-three years. I've had to pretend not to hear things, not see things, not be able to do things, things that society dictates I should not be able to hear, see, or do."

"Can you imagine what could have happened if you had embraced your gifts instead of shunning them?"

"I would be dead." Lumen pointed to Melahem. "They would have hunted me down and killed me. Not that it matters now."

"Because you are different," I said.

"Yes. They would have seen me as a threat and not someone who had too wild of an imagination as a child."

"There. You have just summed up what brought the ultimate destruction upon Earth. Humans and fear are the deadliest combination. Your power could have saved them."

"What power?" Lumen snarled. His Light was flickering and turning red with anger again. "I've been cursed my entire life. I hear voices of people who are not there. I see people I know to be dead, people whose bodies I've watched burn. How is that not a curse?"

I walked obrt and grabbed his hand, then pulled him to the ground and shoved his fingers deep into the sand until we reached living earth.

"Close your eyes," I said. "Do you feel it?"

"Feel what?" he snapped.

"Energy, power, life. Concentrate. Dig deeper until you feel it. I am not helping you this time, like I helped you feel the energy of the beasts the first night that we were in the desert. You have the power to conjure the energy on your own."

Lumen shook his head in disbelief. I pushed his hand down farther, until nearly his entire forearm was buried. That's when I saw it: his red Light had changed to a deep swirling purple. I watched as Lumen's soul grew until it no longer a light flickering in the center of his being, it was larger than him. It reached up to the heavens and down to the roots of the Earth. It swirled around him, purple and white light, like a galaxy.

He pulled his arm out of the ground, clutching a fist full of soil that, after a few seconds, he allowed to slowly slip from his grasp. As the soil spilled from his hand, his Light dissipated.

I could see his chest rise and fall as he breathed deep. His eyes were wide, his pupils dilated. He looked both shaken and exhilarated.

"You have to embrace your power, what you are capable of," I said. "If you embrace it, you can learn to control it. When you fear something, that is when it takes over, possessing your mind and body. When you fear something, it owns you."

"Sometimes fear can save you," Lumen shot back.

"The only fear that can save you is the fear of fear itself," I said. "Every other fear does nothing but make you weak."

Lumen stood silent, gaping at me. I began to walk away from him and towards the city.

"I am not weak," Lumen stuttered his words. His feet fell heavy against the ground behind me as he jogged to catch up.

"Prove it then," I replied.

I had watched countless men declare their strength and shout to the stars that they were fearless. It was never long after their declaration that the very fear they had dismissed brought their downfall upon them.

I had watched the minds of men destroy far more lives than all floods, hurricanes, and fires combined.

Lumen never replied to challenge, and we continued to walk on in silence. I stole a glance at his face: it was pensive, as though he was thinking over my words and the events that he had just witnessed.

Standing face-to-face with the devil was a lot to recover from, especially for a human who had just learned that he, in fact, was not completely human and was seen as a trophy for the devil to win.

Night began to fall as we marched towards Melahem. We did not stop in the middle of the desert to rest. Lumen was still exhilarated from the rush of energy that had filled his body when we were up on the cliff, and so we were able to push on. The last visible hue of sunlight was swallowed by a thick cloud when the ground began to quake. A trumpet's call echoed through the desert.

"The second trumpet." I said.

The ground continued to shake and the sky over Melahem turned deep red. Fire illuminated a sight that caused my stomach to clench in horror: six crosses were standing on the edge of the desert, between us and the city.

THE SECOND TRUMPET

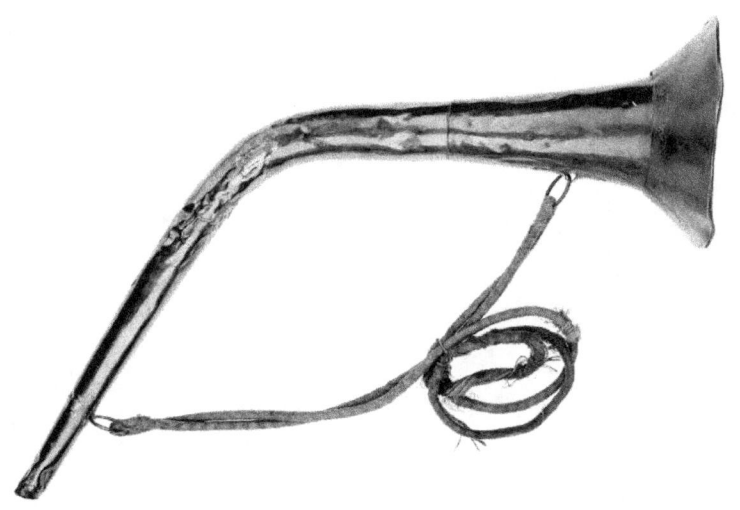

CHAPTER SIX

Once my eyes adjusted to the light, I could see the volcano spewing lava into the air. I walked with Lumen up to the crosses. I could see the curiosity on his face as we approached, but I already had an inkling of what was to be revealed.

The closer we crept to the crosses, the lighter I began to step. As the grains of sand crunched beneath my boot, I felt as though I was disturbing a holy place, a patch of land marked in memory of a disaster. A place where memories, prayers, and offerings were extended to the deceased in hopes of bringing peace and rest to their souls—or at least to lighten the hearts of the offerers.

When we were close enough to clearly see the display erected at the edge of the city, I had to look away. I recognized all six faces of the crucified. They were the content, hardworking family that I had observed in the house with the sideways door.

Lumen's entire family was hanging up on the wooden structures with nails through their hands and overlapped feet. They were taken before they possessed any Light in their souls, before they had any hope of salvation.

Lumen fell to his knees screamed. Lava froze in midair. The world was silent. Everything was still, except for the two of us.

I watched as his body was consumed by his energy. Purple and white bolts of electricity swirled around him, accompanied by a red flame that burned bright. I knelt down beside him and placed a hand on his shoulder.

"I know who gave you your power," I said in awe. Even angels did not possess the power to stop time.

Lumen glared at me with red, burning eyes.

"The Creator," I continued, "shared their power with you. They have hope for humanity yet."

"The Creator?" Lumen roared. "The Almighty Creator that would not allow you to save my family?"

"Lumen," I started in an attempt to comfort him, but I was at a loss for words. Lucifer had stepped over the line. He had broken the reaping code. I was supposed to have until the seventh trumpet's blow to gather all of the innocent souls that I could before Lucifer was set loose on the planet. And while Lumen's family was not innocent, there was always a chance that he could have turned them in time.

"Do not let Lucifer win you over," I said.

"He took my family," shouted Lumen. "Are they all in Hell now? Is there no chance of saving them?"

"If they changed their Light before he took them, they will be Home," I said. "Seeing you now, though, I believe that there may be hope for all of the lost."

"How?" He turned away from his family to look at me. Tears stained his face.

"You have the ability to control time," I said. "That is a power that even I do not possess."

As Lumen took in a deep breath and let it out slowly, the world began to move again, as if it had never paused.

Lava spewed into the night sky once more, lighting the city with fire. I pulled Lumen to his feet. We needed to care for his lost loved ones.

I led him to them, feeling sorrow and pain as I saw him looking up at his murdered family. He was alone in the world now. In my years, I have seen a lost man's path go two ways: either he allowed the sorrow to consume and destroy him, or he relished in it and was reborn from the pyre ashes. I prayed that Lumen would be reborn and use all of his power to save not only them, but the rest of souls of the Earth.

I looked again at my brother's handiwork. It was a stomach-turning sight, as had been many pages of Earth's history when Lucifer had played in the destruction of humanity. Lucifer thrived on war. He loved how easy humans were for him to manipulate. Their minds were different from any other people in the universe; they were more malleable. This had been done with the intention of them being the most innocent of all, but Lucifer had taken full advantage of their free will and manipulated their minds.

I pulled the crosses from the ground one by one and rested them on the ground. I used my magic to pull the nails from each of the family members' hands and feet. Gently, we lifted their bodies from the crosses and laid them next to each other. Lumen helped me break down the crosses into firewood, pulling the nailed pieces apart with his bare hands. We stacked the large wooden planks side by side, and two planks high. Carefully, I helped Lumen carry the bodies over and tenderly place them on the stacked wood.

Tears continued to flow down Lumen's face as we prepared to return their bodies to ash, and I could see the red flame still burning bright in the place of his white Light.

I began the prayer.

"Dear Creator, a misdeed was done to these good people and another was left to suffer. I pray that their souls find their way into your home, and that you guide us on the journey that you have intended. I see hope for these people yet, and we will continue to fight on their behalf."

I conjured up a flame in my right hand and looked at Lumen. He nodded that he was ready.

"Until that time, I set these people free of the world and of what has yet to come. Ashes to ashes and dust to dust," I finished my prayer.

I walked around the pyre and lit a flame at the head of each of Lumen's family members, then at their feet.

We stood together watching the bodies burn to ash. They neither glowed nor floated through the night sky. Lumen did not seem to notice the difference between the ashes of his family and the Waters', so I let him have his peace.

Once the flame had burnt out, I put up a barrier around us and sparked a small campfire. I was sure that the scent of burning flesh would attract unwanted guests, but Lumen deserved time to mourn, and I knew that he would not be able to complete our walk through the city that night.

"Everything that is happening right now," Lumen said, looking at the pile of ash that was once his family, "it is all because of fear?"

"Yes," I replied. "Fear of the unknown. Humans continually destroyed themselves in their fear of what they did not understand. Some tried to understand, or to pull others away from Lucifer's path, but they were shunned."

"The witches," said Lumen.

"Yes, the witches, the prophets, the innocent who still possessed the ability to see past this world," I said. "But they were all deemed insane, or evil, by others who no longer possessed those powers."

"It doesn't really make sense, does it? Fear, that is."

"No, it does not. I never fully understood it. Fear is irrational," I said. "I once watched a man burn down his entire house in an attempt to kill a spider that was smaller than a pebble. He almost died and lost everything that he owned because he allowed fear to take over."

"What is a spider?"

"They were an animal called arachnids. Many were small, smaller than the nail of your baby finger." I looked down at my fingernail. I drew a circle in the sand with eight lines coming from the center, then held my hand over the sketching and pulled enough energy from the Earth to bring the creature to life; a small brown spider with a speckled body and oversized skinny legs climbed up into the palm of my hand. "Their bodies were small in proportion to their legs, which were long for climbing. They kept to themselves and ate insects, but they were feared by many."

"Why would people fear something so small?" asked Lumen. He held his hand up to mine and allowed the creature to crawl onto it. "And why don't we have spiders in Melahem?"

"Because they cannot survive here," I said. "Every plant and animal that exists in Melahem is a mutation of what once was. The pollution is too great here for any pure creature to survive."

I took the spider back into my hand, blew on it, and turned it back to dust.

"You said that there is still a chance that I could save my family," said Lumen. "How can I do that?"

"You can either control your fear or you can allow your fear to control you," I said. "You need to harness the power that lives within you. You have the ability to stop time; I believe you may possess the ability to reverse it as well."

"You think I could go back in time and save my family?" His eyes were wide with hope.

"I believe that you could go back in time and save Earth. You could save the people, the animals, the plants," I said. "I believe that you are the key to saving humanity."

"How?" His voice sounded excited and empowered. "How do I save everyone?"

"I will help you learn to control your power," I said. "For now, though, you should rest. We will begin tomorrow."

Lumen followed my instruction, but I knew that sleep would not come easy for him. His mind was racing with the possibility of hope, just as mine was.

Mine was, too. I could not help going over Lucifer's proposed deal in my mind.

All of the children. All of the souls that would not last in Hell. They would be broken and beaten. They would be used to fuel the flames. I could not bring myself to think of the children that my brother had already laid claim to.

He knew that the children of Earth had a special place in my soul, being the closest thing to holy that the planet ever was blessed with after the crucifixion, innocent and pure.

All that I could do was pray that I was not reading the signs wrong. I needed Lumen to be the answer that could save Earth. The answer that could save the children.

CHAPTER SEVEN

I allowed Lumen to sleep until he woke on his own. He was going to need strength and energy if he was going to learn to control his powers.

We walked through the heart of the city and made our way to the water. The smell of rotting flesh filled the air from the carcasses of fish, mutated whales and dolphins, and other unrecognizable creatures that blanketed the shoreline. The people of the city were desperately sorting through the bodies for any salvageable meat, but it was all rotten.

Lumen covered his face with his shirt. The smell was inducing vomiting in the village people around us, and the sight was gruesome enough to turn even the strongest of stomachs.

"I want to help," said Lumen in a muffled voice through his shirt. He was looking out at what was left of a once great sea at the sun reflecting off the scales of hundreds of thousands of rotted fish.

The carcasses crashed into each other, piling up on the shoreline. Fishermen and other folks from the city were working together to create burn piles.

The sight reminded me of dump sites and garbage piles from an earlier Earth. Piles of unwanted goods and spoiled food would burn day and night. The smell was vile, and the sight of so much waste was even more so.

"There is nothing that you can do for these people at the moment," I said. "Let them burn the corpses. We have much other work to do."

Lumen followed me as I led him through the city, searching for souls. I could not feel any Light pulling me in its direction, so I wandered in hopes of stumbling upon even the weakest of glimmers.

Eventually, I could start to feel a strong Light. As I began following it, I felt another soul, and then another. I could feel the pull coming from every direction.

I stopped and closed my eyes and tried to concentrate on just one soul, but they were all blurring into each other.

"Something is wrong," I said to Lumen.

Just past the outer edge of the city, I saw it: a large tree. People were crowded around it, dancing and singing. Some looked as though they were dying, but no one stopped the help them. They just stepped over the bodies and continued on their way.

"What's going on?" asked Lumen.

"I am not sure." I replied.

We carefully made our way up to the tree, maneuvering around the mass of people who surrounded it. As we got closer, I could see that it was producing large, apple-shaped fruit with marbled red, green, and black coloring.

"That tree has never produced fruit before," said Lumen.

"That is because it is not the same tree," I said.

I pressed my index finger against the trunk of the tree; the pressure caused a black liquid to ooze out from beneath the bark. It was thick and sticky. Lucifer was playing a game with me. He had planted the Tree of the Knowledge of Good and Evil right in the heart of the city, knowing it would interfere with my reaping, as I would not be able to tell an innocent soul from an infected one.

"Blood," I said.

"Blood?" repeated Lumen. "The tree is bleeding?"

"It is rooted in Hell," I said. "This is the tree that possesses the knowledge of good and evil. It was humanity's first downfall. He is mocking us."

"The tree possesses knowledge of good and evil? How is that possible?"

"Biting into the fruit opens one's mind to see everything from before they lost their innocence," I said. "It is going to cause them to all seem as if they are filled with the pure light of the innocent, but they are all just going mad. Their minds are being opened to too much truth at one time."

A wild-eyed woman ran between me and Lumen, pushing us to the side. Her face was smudged with dirt and her hair was sticking out in all directions. I could see stains from the juice of the fruit running down her face and arms.

"This is my fruit," she growled. I watched as she gathered as much of the poisoned fruit as she could carry. Then she ran off to a half-burnt building and began shoveling her bounty into her mouth. Juice dripped down her arms and face as her eyes grew more and more wild with every bite. I could see her Light flickering white and purple and red. The poor soul was possessed and dying. There was no hope of saving her.

"She could see you, and she touched you," Lumen observed.

"The fruit is infected with a virus," I said. "It eats away at the mind and opens the darker corners that are best left untouched. She now can see demons and angels walking the earth."

We watched the frenzied people of Melahem. Some began violently shaking and convulsing as the virus took them over. Others screamed and foamed at the mouth while eating even more of the poisoned fruit. A few sat alone with their knees pulled up to their chest, quietly mumbling and rocking back and forth.

48

"We need to destroy the tree," I said. "It is the only way that we will be able to break the poison's spell."

"How do we do that?"

I was not sure how to answer him. Honestly, I was not sure if we would be able to destroy the tree at all. Lucifer had planted its root past the barriers between Hell and Earth. But Lumen needed something to focus on. He needed to learn how to channel his energy if there was any hope of saving the people of Melahem.

"We need to go back out to the desert," I said. "It is time to teach you how to control your power. I am going to need your help if we are going to be successful in destroying this tree."

Lumen did not argue. He followed me through the city, past all of his neighbors who were beginning to lose control of their minds. They stumbled into us. One seemed drunk as he fell into my arms. I had to push him back up onto his feet. I watched as he continued to walk with unstable balance, falling and crawling his way up to the tree. It felt odd being in the middle of a group of people who could see me and touch me. I knew that they would not follow us out to the desert, though. They would not stray far from the tree and its fruit. They were becoming addicted to the poison as it ate away at their minds.

People surrounding us were speaking in tongues that should never have been uttered on Earth. They were speaking languages from different planets and different dimensions. Many of them were speaking in the tongue of the devil himself. Lucifer took pride in creating his own language. He called it the holy language. I knew it for what it was, though: nothing more than another childish protest.

At the edge of the city, we walked past a child of no more than five years. He had his knees pulled up towards his chest and he was mumbling a demonic chant in ancient Latin. His soul was swirling in confusion. I bent down to him. His eyes were solid black and his teeth had all grown into fangs.

I reached out to place a hand on the boy's shoulder. He hissed and cursed at me as though he already belonged to Lucifer's army.

"Fake angel," he spat at me in Latin, "you are a disgrace."

I stepped back in surprise at the child's statement.

All of the children. I heard Lucifer's voice echoing through my mind. *What if Lumen could not learn to control his powers? What if Lucifer had planted him here as a test? What if I was wrong, and I was not interpreting the signs properly?*

I closed my eyes and shook my head. I had to push those thoughts out of my mind. I needed to believe that I was making the right decision. I needed to believe that Lumen was the answer.

"Are you all right?" Lumen's voice broke my train of thought. I felt his hand pulling on my shoulder.

"Yes," I replied, "I just ...."

I was not sure how to finish my sentence. I was not sure that I wanted to finish it. I did know that I wanted to get out of the city as quickly as possible, and that I was going to need Lumen's assistance to tear down the tree that had been tormenting humanity since the beginning of the species' existence.

Lumen helped pull me to my feet, away from the poisoned boy, and we walked to the desert. It was comforting to be away from the city. Once we were far enough away that the voices of the poisoned people were just a faint rumble, we settled down. We had walked just past the cliffs that fenced the desert off from the city.

"So," I began, "in order to control your energy and power, you must first learn to control your mind."

I sat down on the sand and crossed my legs. I watched as Lumen copied me, sitting directly in front of me.

"Close your eyes," I instructed. "Take a deep breath, as deep as you can, and let it out slowly."

I watched as Lumen followed my instructions. I also followed my directives and concentrated on Lumen's breathing pattern and heartbeat.

"Keep breathing in and out. Clear your mind," I said. "Feel your heartbeat slow. Let go of everything that is holding you to this land. Observe your thoughts and emotions. Free yourself from them."

This had always been the most difficult part of training for me when I was learning to control my magic. It took me years to conquer my rage and become neutral in the lives of the Creator's beings. In all honesty, I do not believe that I ever gained full command of my anger. It was always burning deep in the pit of my stomach, but it drove me to where I an today. I refused to be completely empty, and although that was against our code, against my training, I believe that the Maker admired that about me. I never broke the laws, or Their orders, but I refused to let go of my own thoughts and ideas. I felt a connection to every planet. I could feel it killing me and reviving me every day.

I listened to Lumen's breathing. His heartrate had slowed significantly. He was breathing deeply and expelling his anger with every exhale.

"Good," I said. "Now I want you to concentrate on the fruit tree that grows outside of your family home. Picture it in your mind. Feel its bark, its leaves. Taste the fruit that it produces."

I could see Lumen's eyes rapidly moving behind his eyelids.

"Become so close to the tree that you could reach out and touch it from right here in the desert," I instructed. "Plant your hands deep into the earth. Feel the energy of the tree flowing to you. Concentrate on its roots. They are connected to everything on this planet, just as you are."

I watched as Lumen focused. His breathing was beginning to speed up again. His breaths were shallow and his heat was beating faster than it had been when we first started the exercise. He could not feel the energy of the tree, and he was starting to panic.

"Control your breathing," I coached.

His Light was flickering red and white as he became more and more frustrated. It was going to take more time than I had expected to train Lumen to control his mind, let alone his magic. I hoped it wouldn't take more time than Melahem could afford.

The red flame in his soul was beginning to overtake the white. His breathing was becoming heavier with every breath.

"Lumen." I reached out and placed a hand on his arm. He dug his hands deeper into the desert sand. His face twisted in pain as he let out a scream that echoed through the grey air.

I pulled his hands from the ground. His eyes shot open. I could see the frustration on his face.

"I couldn't feel the tree," he whispered.

"It will take time and practice," I said.

"We don't have time," Lumen protested. "We need to destroy the tree."

"We will," I said in a convincing tone. Where was that power that I had seen just the night before? Where was that magic and energy that caused time to stop? Lumen needed to concentrate on his abilities. He needed to let go of all of his fears.

"I'm sorry." Lumen looked and sounded devastated.

"Do not be sorry. You just need to practice. And you will need energy to do so."

I closed my eyes and pulled a plant from a memory that I carried with me from the beginning of my training. I summoned us a tree that bore a protein- and vitamin-filled fruit that speckled the forests of Corton. The plant only bloomed and bore fruit in the light of the planet's three moons on a cloudless night, which happened with each of the six seasons. The Cortonians would spend entire nights harvesting the fruit. Those six nights each year were honored with festivals, art, and music. The Cortonians thrived in the darkness; they worshiped it.

"What is this?" Lumen asked. He plucked a fruit from the tree and took a large bite from it.

"*Du Lìv de Nōc*," I replied.

"What?" His face was screwed up in confusion.

Lumen forced himself to swallow the bite of fruit he had taken.

"The life of the night," I translated. "It is a holy fruit from the planet

Corton. It is very healthy and it will reenergize you."

"It doesn't taste like it," said Lumen. He looked down at the black and white speckled fruit in disgust.

"Eat. You expended a lot of energy last night, and you will be using even more today," I said.

I plucked a fruit from the crooked plant that clearly did not belong on Earth. Tall, with jagged limbs, it had thorns that were over an inch in length. The thorns protected red blossoms that resembled a leaf more than a flower. The blossoms produced large black fruit with white speckles. Looking into the fruit reminded me of the harvest night's sky on Corton.

I took a bite. The juices made the inside of my cheeks tingle as they rolled down the back of my tongue. The fruit was not sweet, nor bitter. It had its own unique flavor, like rosehip tea infused with tart berries and lavender. I found the taste intoxicating.

Once we had both finished eating, I sent the tree back into the earth.

"Come," I said. I rubbed the desert sand off of my hands. "It is time for your next lesson."

Lumen followed me obediently out of the desert and back through Melahem. I was not excited to return to the city so soon, but Lumen required something material to concentrate on. He was not yet ready to connect to the earth through energy alone. I led him to the edge of the city to a pile of half-burnt fish carcasses. It was growing late in the day, and many of the city's residents had begun hiding from the putrid smell of burnt and rotting flesh—those who had not yet become infected by the tree, that is.

"What are we doing out here?" asked Lumen.

He held his hands over his nose and mouth, shielding them from the stench that was so strong it stuck to the back of my tongue. .

"You are going to finish burning this mountain of fish."

"I don't have a match or flint rock," he replied.

"You will not require any," I assured him.

Lumen needed something that was physically in front of him to focus his energy on. He'd been consumed by anger and rage when he was able to stop time. Now I was going to teach him to funnel his anger toward my brother

"Look at this pile of waste," I said. "These fish were your family's livelihood. Lucifer took that away from you, just as he did your family. He destroyed your food source and the jobs of your neighbors. Lucifer took the lives of these animals, just as he did your family. Slaughtered and wasted."

I could see Lumen's face growing red at my words. I needed him to be consumed by anger. I needed him to focus all of his energy on my brother.

I closed my eyes and focused on Lucifer. I pictured his face in my mind. I could almost feel his lifeless eyes staring into my own and see the black veins pulsing on his neck and forehead.

I pulled the image from my mind and pasted it on the pile mountain of bodies. An illusion, a hologram of Lucifer's face flickered on the corpses, taunting Lumen.

I could see the bright red fire burning in Lumen's soul. His hands shook at the sight of my brother.

"He took your family from you," I went on. "He destroyed your home. He has driven the people of your city mad with forbidden fruit and they are tearing the city down brick by brick."

"No," Lumen's voice was shaky. His body was quivering with anger. "No, no, no."

He repeated the word over and over, his voice becoming louder and more forceful with every utterance.

I watched in awe as Lumen closed his eyes and let out a roar. He shook the earth again, as he'd done when he first laid eyes on his crucified family.

His hands became engulfed in flames. They burned bright, two torches, the color of his soul.

He threw his hands out in front of himself and fire erupted in a solid stream. It flew through the air and landed in the center of the hologram of Lucifer's face.

I watched the face melt as the mound of bodies disintegrated in front of us.

Lumen did not stop with the one pile of fish, but pushed his fury into the surrounding piles, five in total, until we were surrounded by mountains of fire.

Lumen's body resembled more a living flame than a human being. Flames danced in his eyes.

I followed Lumen as he strode to the shoreline and waded out into the tide that was still shoveling bodies up on to the beach. He dropped his hands into the water and set the ocean on fire. The flame spread much more quickly than I had expected. In a matter of seconds, the entire sea was burning around Lumen who stood, untouched by the fire he had created, admiring his work.

After what seemed like hours, he turned around and walked back to me on the shore. The burning bodies parted to either side of Lumen, allowing him to pass without coming into contact with the fish. By the time he reached the land, the flames had left his body. He was breathing heavily and drenched in sweat.

"Lumen," I said, "that was incredible."

"I can do this," he panted. "I can help you save my family and the rest of Melahem."

"Yes," I agreed. "I do believe you can."

I had misjudged; Lumen was not going to take weeks of extra training. He just needed the proper coaching to trigger and use his power. We sat down on an open bit of sand on the beach and watched as Lumen's handiwork burned around us.

CHAPTER EIGHT

We sat in silence. With the thought of what we were actually looking at pushed aside, it was a beautiful sight: a glowing sea of black, orange, and red, flowing back and forth under the light of the high burning flames that surrounded us.

It reminded me of the lava seas that had consumed the planet before the waters and land were created. Earth had been a beautiful burning ball of crackling, spewing fire. I'd loved to sit and watch the way the colors swirled.

"We have to destroy that tree." Lumen broke my reminiscing. "We have to kill it tonight."

"Don't need to rest after using all that energy?" I asked. "I would not object if you require sleep before we take down the tree. It will require much more energy than these flames that you conjured."

"I can do it," said Lumen. He looked around at the towers of flames that surrounded us. "I know that I can help. I know how to help you now. I can feel it. The connection that you were telling me about between myself and the earth, I can feel the energy pulsing through me now. I can feel the earth."

"Are you sure?" I asked. "What you feel could still be from the energy you used to conjure the flames."

I believed that adrenaline was still rushing through his body and that was why he felt prepared to take on the Tree of the Knowledge of Good and Evil. If he was willing, though, I did want to get close to the tree again. I needed to learn more about what Lucifer had done to the tree in order to destroy it.

"No," he stated firmly. "This is different. I feel in control of my emotions now. I know that I have to focus on my anger. I need to focus on stopping Lucifer."

I nodded in agreement. He *had* gained significant control over his emotions. We were also short on time. Even if we were able to take down the tree that the night, it was too late to save many of the infected people of Melahem. The poison of the fruit was already eating away at their minds, opening more portions of their brains than any human was prepared to handle.

I've always found it interesting just how much power had been given the humans. There were so many areas of their brains that they were never able to unlock. It was almost like Creator was teasing them, dangling a carrot of knowledge and power in front of them, but never swinging it quite within reach.

The Maker's choice that they could not access their full capacity was not a bad thing, in my estimation. Humans has done enough damage with the small fraction of their brain that they were in control of.

Lumen and I rose from the sand and took one last look out at the burning sea. Lumen dusted the wet sand from his clothes and we began our trek back to the city.

The fruit had begun to truly take its toll on the people. We passed a number of people who were foaming at the mouth, their eyes rolled back with only the whites showing. They were convulsing as the poison ate away at their mind, and they had begun to lose control over their bodies.

Others were stronger, able to handle the new sections of their brain as they were unlocked. I could only imagine the fireworks display that must have been going in within their skulls as their synapses fired back and forth.

I spotted the woman with the fried hair who had rushed past Lumen and me earlier in the day. She was stronger than I had assumed, and was in control of her power. I watched as she picked up large stones with only her mind and hurled them at the top of the tree in an attempt to knock down more of the fruit.

We waded through the people and eventually arrived at the tree.

"Are you sure that you are ready for this?" I asked Lumen.

He nodded and closed his eyes. I could see the strain in his face as he concentrated on his energy and his emotions.

Small flames sparked on Lumen's fingertips. I was impressed with the control that he was displaying over his magic.

I closed my eyes and concentrated on my own energy. I pulled everything I could from the soil. There was not much, but it would have to do. I gathered what I could into a swirling purple ball of electricity and threw it straight into the heart of the tree.

My energy ball stopped a few inches before hitting the trunk of the tree. Lucifer had erected walls and protective spells around his creation. This was a new development; they hadn't been there the first time we had come into contact with the tree.

As I stared at my energy suspended in midair, the wall began to react. It pulsed and shot the energy ball directly back at me.

"Move," I screamed. Lumen was standing to my right, and I pushed him to the ground and laid my body on top of his. I could feel the heat from the energy as it passed over us.

I looked up in time to see a large building crumble to the ground after being hit by the energy ball. Stones cascaded down over the people around it. The sight was saddening, but I consoled myself with the thought that the people who died would no longer have to suffer from

Lucifer's games.

"What was that?" asked Lumen.

"Lucifer anticipated my attack against the tree. He's fighting back."

I sat up on my knees and examined the situation. There were no visible barriers around the tree. The people who were eating the fruit plucked it straight from the branches. They could touch it and sit under it with their backs up against the trunk. As I looked closely, I realized that the trunk did not look the same as it had earlier in the day.

I heaved myself up to my feet, and Lumen followed close behind. With every step I took toward the tree, I could feel something trying to keep me away, a magnetic barrier pushing against me. Each step was more and more difficult to take.

I looked to my right and saw Lumen walking with ease at my side. Apparently I was the only one Lucifer did not want coming in contact with his masterpiece.

When I was almost close enough to reach out and touch the trunk of the tree, I found myself unable to take another step and my arms felt as though they were glued to my sides.

I watched as Lumen was able to walk up to the tree and place his hand against it.

"It's soft," he reported, rubbing his hand up and down the trunk. "Like feathers."

I looked closely and discovered it really was made of feathers. Black feathers that ruffled then smoothed again under Lumen's hand.

Feathers? This tree has never been made of feathers. It has always been hard, oozing bark.

Lumen wrapped his fingers around one of the feathers and plucked it from the tree. When he did, the ground quaked and a bolt of lightning shot from tree where the feather had been. It hit Lumen, driving back, and he fell hard to the ground. I pushed and attempted to run to his side, but I was still unable to break though the barrier Lucifer had erected.

"Lumen," I shouted.

He did not move. I was too far away to tell if he was breathing.

I felt anger rising within me. I wanted nothing more than to end my brother's reign of terror over the shambles that were left of Earth. I pushed my power through the ground and focused on Lumen's unmoving body.

I opened my eyes to see tiny pieces of the ground moving, rippling like waves. I pulled him with all my might, his body riding the undulating dirt until he was past both me and the invisible barrier.

As I approached, I could see burn marks from the lightning bolt running up and down his body and clothes.

"Lumen," I said. I shook his shoulders, but he did not respond. I could see his eyes moving behind their lids, so I knew that he was alive.

I gently scooped his head up onto my left arm and pushed my right under his legs. I did not have much energy left, but I knew that we could not stay in the middle of the city.

I forced my body upright with Lumen in my arms and began threading my way back to the desert. It was a long, slow walk, but none of the infected people stopped to bother us; they were more concerned with consuming as much fruit as they could shovel into their mouths.

I barely made it out past the city before my legs gave out and my body collapsed to the ground. I placed Lumen flat on his back and knelt with my hands buried in the sand. I closed my eyes and opened my mind, praying for any energy that existed in the desert to help rejuvenate my own.

I emptied my mind and allowed the energy of the earth to find me. The process was slow, but gradually I could feel my energy being replenished. I could see it flowing through the center of the planet, spreading out like electric roots that connected me to the core of the universe.

I felt refreshed, as though I had awakened from a long nap. I could feel the energy surging through me. I must have been connected to the ground for at least an hour before I had absorbed enough power to get back up on my feet.

As I stood and stretched, I felt a tingling sensation running through my body.

I looked at Lumen. He was still laying in the same position I'd placed him in, and was still breathing. I touched the side of his face. His skin was cold; I had not been aware of the temperature falling while I was pulling energy to myself.

I started a small fire to help warm him, and used my energy to heal the burns the tree had inflicted on his body.

I could still hear the roar from Melahem echoing on the night air.

I pulled my energy from the earth and formed a small dome around Lumen; it would help to rejuvenate his body, but I needed to leave him to rest in the dome long enough for him to absorb its full power.

I looked around and saw a tall cliff that overlooked the city. It would do me good to walk and clear my mind for a bit. Then I needed to figure out how to destroy the tree. Lumen would be safe under the protective dome until my return.

It was not a far walk. From the cliff, I could see the city to my left and Lumen to my right. I knew that nothing could get through the dome, but I was still nervous that Lucifer might attempt to move on Lumen while he was out of my physical reach.

I focused my attention on the city below me, knowing that the fruit affected no two people in the same manner.

I stood watching as the people of Melahem tore each other apart.

I watched as one man began building a beautiful sculpture of the tree using rocks, twigs, and clay. The sculpture was even more beautiful to look at than the tree was.

Others began spewing knowledge at passersby. Some spoke of planets, astrology that no human had ever discovered. Others rattled off facts about technology that was obliterated in the last world war.

The ones that truly caught my eye were the ones who had unlocked special abilities within themselves, abilities they could not control or understand. One woman I had passed by on the streets once before was now setting fire to everything she looked at.

A man made the earth quake whether he moved or stood still. Buildings crumbled around him and the waves of the ocean began to rise.

A small few unlocked something even darker still. They had transformed, becoming more demon then human. They were strong and blood hungry. I watched as they tore limbs off their neighbors while they were still alive and ate the raw flesh off of the bone. Blood dripped down their faces. They licked the spilled blood from their fingers like children eating melting ice cream cones.

I surveyed the situation in horror, searching in my mind for any solution other than exterminating all of the infected.

I felt a presence behind me. I could almost feel the edges of my brother's mouth curl into a tight smile.

"Admiring your work?" I asked. I kept my eyes fixed on the disaster below.

"Yes, the view from afar does not do it justice," Lucifer sneered. "It is quite the masterpiece."

I refused to acknowledge his comment.

"Don't you miss the days when we used to work together, sister?"

"Every day," I admitted.

Lucifer and I used to be a perfect team. We worked together with precision and accuracy. Before Lucifer's fall, we were partners, archangels who fought for peace and for all that is holy.

We trained together, we pushed each other. I knew where he was going to move before he ever took a step and he knew the same for me. We were twins, after all, and shared that special bond.

The greatest pain I had ever felt was the day of Lucifer's descent to Hell. I could feel his anger, his pain, his betrayal. I could feel the flames biting around him. It is a feeling that has never fully gone away. I can always feel his presence, even when we are on completely different sides of the universe. Or different sides of the battle.

"Where is your pet?"

"Safe from your monsters," I said.

"I thought you said you were not going to interfere," said Lucifer.

He stepped up beside me, coming so close our shoulders were almost touching. I glanced at him. He was standing with his hands behind his back, leaning slightly forward, with a grin on his face. He looked like a pleased king.

"I am not interfering. I am following The Plan," I said.

"The Plan?" Lucifer exclaimed. "What authority do you have to interpret The Plan for any planet? Especially this one?"

"I have more authority than you, brother," I responded.

"And if you are wrong?" he sneered.

"Then you win. Why do you show such an interest in this?" I could feel my anger toward my brother rising.

"What good brother does not show an interest in the potential failure of his *perfect* sister?" Lucifer snapped back at me.

He put an emphasis on the word perfect that I did not appreciate.

"'Good brother,'" I said with a laugh, "why do you feel the need to torment the humans? Why did you murder Lumen's family?"

My voice grew louder with every word and I was shaking as I turned towards him. I wanted so badly to hurt him as he had hurt so many. I wished that, even if only for a moment, he could feel all the pain he had caused over the millennia.

I could not physically hurt him, though, just as he could not physically hurt me. In all of our years, we had never been able to injure each other, although we'd tried. It was something that had happened before our birth into the material plane. Something that I did not understand. It was never explained and, to my knowledge, has not happened to any other angelic siblings since.

All I know is that there is a prophecy of the good and evil in darkness. It is said that these two entities exist to keep balance in the universe. Years ago, long before Earth, I decided that my brother and I fulfilled this prophecy. I needed to believe it. And now more than ever, I needed an explanation for my brother's unleashing of horror and destruction throughout the universe.

"You know why," Lucifer said.

I could see fire and smoke erupting in Melahem as a building crumbled reflected in Lucifer's glass-like eyes.

"Leave me," I said through gritted teeth, "so I can clean up your mess."

"You know that I will never truly leave you," he replied. "Consider my offer."

Then he was gone and I was alone on the cliff, staring into an abyss of madness.

I turned to look at Lumen. I wanted to make sure that he was still where I had left him. I did not know what other tricks Lucifer might have been up to. He was still there, sleeping under the purple dome.

The air was chillier still as the sun descended over the horizon. I descended from the cliff and stopped halfway between it and Lumen. I sat in the cooling sand. I picked up a handful and felt the sun's heat on my palm.

I could hear the people of Melahem behind me, filling the air with shrill screams.

I shoved my fingers in my hair and clenched my hands into fists at the roots. I tugged hard out of frustration, perhaps hoping to pull the answer to my current situation out of my mind.

I closed my eyes to meditate, but I could still see the scene from the cliff replaying. I could still hear Lucifer's voice in my mind.

For the first time I could remember, I was not sure what to do.

I was not sure how to destory the tree. I was not sure it *could* be destroyed.

I was not sure what to do with the infected people. My first thought was to extinguish them, at least the ones that had turned to cannibalism, but I refused to play into Lucifer's hand. There had to be a way to save them, at least some of them, but I did not have the answer.

I shoved my hand deep into the sand and allowed the energy of the earth to consume me. I gave my mind away to the power that fused the universe together.

I felt my connection to every tree, plant, and fruit in existence. Nothing matched what I had felt when I was near Lucifer's tree.

I decided that instead of trying to find a connection between the Tree of Knowledge and a similar plant, I should connect directly to the poison bearing tree.

I siphoned my own energy out, through the earth, to the tree. I did not feel anything in return. I pushed deeper into the ground, searching for any sign of it. If I could touch just a spark of the tree's energy, I could potentially learn how to destroy it.

I pushed down until my entire forearm was buried in the sand before I could finally feel *something*. It was faint, but it was there. I pushed down a little farther. I was close.

A scorching flame rushed through the particles of the earth. It engulfed my arm and pulled me down until my arm was buried up to my shoulder.

I pressed against ground, attempting to pull myself free. I could feel my flesh burning.

I grabbed my buried arm with my free hand to help pull it up, but the skin of my shoulder was boiling and the skin of my hand began melting to the skin of my shoulder. When I pulled my hand away, the flesh of my shoulder tore away with it, revealing bare bone.

Tears were rolling down my face as I screamed in pain. I collapsed to the ground, shaking. I could feel the energy pulsing through me as my arm burned. I could feel shocks and sparks tingling through my bones. I did not have the strength, nor the energy, to continue the fight. The pain had overwhelmed me. I felt paralyzed.

As I took a shaking breath of defeat, my arm was suddenly free of the energy. I kept my position on the desert floor for another minute before I forced myself to pull my arm from the sand.

It was untouched. I looked at my shoulder. It was just as it was before I had submerged my arm.

It had all been just a mind game. The tree fed me illusions. Lucifer was playing one of his tricks on me.

I sat with my knees pulled up to my chest, still shaking from the horror I had been tricked into believing I was experiencing.

I took another deep breath. I still felt as though my arm was on fire. I could still *feel* the tree.

All at once, I realized what I needed to do. I knew how to kill it.

CHAPTER NINE

I sat up for an hour before I could move again. My body and mind felt weak. This wasn't one of Lucifer's typical games. He had delved into a different level of dark magic. He had covered the trunk of the Tree of the Knowledge of Good and Evil with the wings of fallen angels.

There's a special kind of darkness that lives in expelled angels, so much hatred and evil. Every angel has free will, just as the humans. Everyone, including Lucifer, was able to walk away from Home at any moment that they pleased, but it took a special kind of darkness to be expelled from the abode of a forgiving parent.

The wings that protected the tree were from those who not only chose to follow my brother into Hell, but also committed unforgivable acts of evil that revoked their right to step foot into Heaven.

Lucifer's angels. He'd plucked their wings and dyed them black. He'd hung them on the walls of his inferno as gruesome trophies. He then replaced their glorious strong wings with his own creation of bone and flesh from the victims that he had laid claim to.

The angelic wings that he'd collected still held significant power. Angels who had not fallen were forbidden from interacting with the ones who had. We could not even approach them. The only exception to this rule was my brother and me. We were a different sort of team, and he was a different class of evil.

When I'd connected with the tree's energy, I'd recognized the strength and power that was keeping me away from it. Me attempting to approach the tree was like trying to push two magnets of the same charge together—there is a natural and proper force keeping them apart, and they will never come into contact with each other.

Lucifer had known that if he wrapped the tree in the wing feathers of the fallen angels, I would not be able to approach it. He had, of course, also coated the tree in magic and spells that would deflect any person who could touch the tree from harming it.

What Lucifer forgot, though, is that everything is connected. Everything on the shambles of Earth to the thriving planets on the other side of the universe, they are all connected. If I could siphon enough energy, I could break his barrier. The answer was in the roots; they are both the strongest and weakest point of any plant. They are what holds the tree to the ground, what makes it stand tall, but if the roots were tampered with, Lucifer's tree could fall just as any other, their connection to Hell notwithstanding.

I felt a rush of adrenaline as I realized I had the answer. My brother was clever, but he was always more concerned with appearances than the end game. Maybe that was why he enjoyed the humans so much. They had plenty in common.

I pushed myself to my feet. I could still feel the energy of the tree surging through me, and it was difficult for me to keep my balance. Although I left no marks on the ground, I could still feel my feet slipping beneath the loose grains of sand. I slid with every step that I took. I had to use my hands to keep from tumbling.

I was excited to tell Lumen what I had discovered. I was going to need his help, because although I could interfere with the tree's root system, I still could not touch the tree itself. Lumen was going to need to be able to use his power to battle the visible portions of the tree and to tear the wings from its trunk.

As I approached, Lumen rose quickly and walked to meet me as close to the edge of the dome as he could get. He looked worried.

When I passed through the dome, the energy loosened, forming a doorway for me to enter. Once I was through, the hole was patched with impenetrable energy again.

"Where have you been?" asked Lumen. His voice was frantic.

I sat down next to the fire.

"Come sit." I motioned to the ground next to me. I was happy to see that he was well and awake.

Lumen's face showed his irritation at me for leaving him alone, trapped in the dome. He came and sat beside me, but did not look at me. Instead, he gazed into the fire.

"I know how to destroy the tree," I said.

He was silent for a moment before he said, "I thought that your magic did not work on the tree."

"It does not," I affirmed. "But yours will."

"What magic do I possess?" Lumen said, his voice bitter. "I can't even start my own bonfire without you pulling it out of me, let alone destroy a poison-spewing tree that is rooted in Hell!"

"You tore a feather from the tree. You made it bleed. That is more than I can do," I said. "I will continue to help you practice. I believe in you."

"Why is the tree covered in feathers now?"

"My brother decided to cover the tree in the wings of fallen angels. That is why I cannot touch the tree," I replied.

"The wings of fallen angels? How did you find that out?"

"I felt it. I connected with the energy of the tree," I said. "Angels who have not fallen are unable to interact with those who have. Not only is it forbidden, there are magics in place that make it impossible.

And although they are no longer attached to the angels, the wings still hold enough power to keep me at a distance.

"I cannot touch the tree, but in order for it to survive here it has to be connected to the rest of the planet, so I was able to reach it through its root system. The main root of the tree is rooted in Hell, but it has spread out across Melahem as well.

"And while I cannot physically touch the tree, you can. I believe that if you are able to attack it from the outside and I am able to attack it from within, we will be able to destroy the tree for good," I said.

"But what if I can't?" Lumen asked. "It did more damage to me than I did to it."

"You had also used most of your energy burning the piles of fish," I reminded him. "When we go back tomorrow night, we will both be well rested and ready for the battle."

Lumen looked at me wide-eyed. I could tell that he was unsure of his own abilities. His face gave away that he did not share the same faith in himself that I had. He still did not understand the true potential of his power. If I had the proper amount of time needed to train him, Lumen would be able to take down the Tree of Knowledge within minutes, if not seconds, because of the intensity of the power that was alive within him.

"We both need to rest," I said. "We will prepare for what is to come in the morning."

I lowered the flame of the fire and motioned for Lumen to lie back down. I did not want to discuss the tree or what I had experienced any further. I needed to clear my mind and push my brother from my thoughts.

I laid down to rest, wishing I could sleep, but that had never been a luxury that angels were able to experience. We rested and meditated, but we were always awake and aware of our surroundings.

It was beyond imaginging, the terror that would befall an angel caught sleeping if Lucifer or a member of his army was near. Yet I wished for sleep, for the ability to fully empty my mind of all thoughts and worries.

I laid awake, resting through the night, watching as the different shades of grey swirled in the thick, dark air. I could see different hues in the sky as the moon struggled to break through the clouds.

I thought back to hundreds of years before when people could lay down on soft green grasses and look up at the night sky and be mesmerized by the beauty of the stars. Humans used to find hope and meaning in the sky. It brought them a feeling of tranquility and peace. It also made them feel like they had a reason in the world. Looking up at the colorful, swirling sky would give them the sence that the world was so much bigger than the issues that they were surrounded with in their own life, that worries were pointless, that that they could find peace in nature and settle their minds.

Even though the sky was now nowhere near as beautiful as it used to be, it still brought me peace.

Lumen began to stir as the sky brightened. He rolled over onto his side and opened his eyes.

"Do you feel rested?" I asked.

Lumen nodded.

I pulled a variety of fruits from old Earth for Lumen to eat. He was going to need all the strength and energy he could gather before we ventured back out into the city.

I watched as he ate kiwi fruit, apples, and strawberries. I plucked a few strawberries myself and took a bite into one. It was sweet and refreshing. The taste took me back to the beginning on the Earth. Strawberries were one of the first plants created. They were one of my favorite foods. I wished that I could eat more than just a few bites. It was truly delicious.

"When we bring down the tree," I said, "I will only be able to assist you from a distance."

"I know." Lumen's voice was soft. "I'm afraid that I won't be able to make a difference and that the tree will be stronger than me."

"You are more powerful than you know," I said. "The tree will be no match for you."

"I hope so," said Lumen. He took a large bite out of an apple.

"Once we are able to pull the wings from the tree, its power will be cut in half. If you can tear them free we should have enough power between us to burn it down," I said.

"How did Lucifer get the wings of fallen angels?"

"When an angel chooses to go to—or is forced—into Hell, Lucifer plucks their wings. He collects them like trophies. He replaces them with a disturbing combination of bone and tattered flesh. It is his way of mocking our Creator," I explained.

"So why is it that you cannot go near the wings?" asked Lumen.

"Because those angels are cut off. There is a barrier between us and them to ensure their seclusion. Lucifer is the only exception," I said.

"So there is no hope for anyone who gets sent to Hell?" The concerned look on his face told me he was thinking about his unsaved family.

"Actually, there is hope," I told him. "If Lucifer chooses to come back and ask for forgiveness, the others will be allowed the same option."

"Really?" Lumen's face lit up. "Do you think that will ever happen?"

"I do not know," I said honestly. "But there is always hope. Never give up on your faith."

We ate and listened. The poison fruit had to have infected almost, if not all, of the city, if the cacophony was any indication.

"Do not forget that Lucifer is a master of mind games," I warned Lumen. "And do not believe anything you see when you are attacking the tree. He can create illusions and make you think that your body is on fire when he is really only manipulating your mind."

I could feel my body physically recoil as the memory of the illusion I'd experienced the night before washed over me. I ran my hand up and down the arm I'd been tricked into believing was burned.

"Okay." Lumen nodded.

"You are stronger than his illusions; you can fight through them," I said.

"I think I'm ready," he said. "I feel strong, stronger than I ever have."

I nodded in agreement. Being so pressed for time, we had to act quickly. Without another word, we pushed ourselves up off of the sandy surface of the desert and started our journey into Melahem.

As we walked through the city, the stench of the rotting fish was almost too much to bear. I could taste the odor on the back of my tongue, and Lumen covered his face with his shirt to stave off the smell.

People lines the edges of the streets. Some were muttering nonsense, others were attempting to control telekinetic abilities that they were never meant to possess. I watched as one woman used her power to pick up an entire building, but her abilities were not strong enough to hold it, and the structure came crashing down on top of her.

We wove our way through the crowds until we were in sight of the tree.

"I will be here," I said, as I stopped about fifty feet away from our target. I knew that if I were to get closer, the barrier would begin to siphon off my energy.

"I can do this," Lumen said with confidence, then marched determinedly onward.

Colors swirled around the tree as Lumen approached it. I watched as he reached out and touched a wing that was wrapped around the trunk. He slid his hands between the wings and pulled. This time, he was not electrocuted by the tree had been when he plucked a feather from it, but, rather, was greeted by a vision.

Light shot from the branches of the tree and sparks of every color swirled around him. Particles that looked like pieces of glass flew around his body and came together in front of him. The pieces melded together and a human form stood before Lumen.

My eyes grew wide as I saw Lumen's mother appear before him. She did not look like the visions or holograms that I could create. She looked as if she had come back from the grave. If I had not burned her body myself, I would have believed she was real.

"Lumen," she said his name in the same soft voice that I remembered hearing when I had visited their house. She reached out and cupped his left cheek in her hand. I watched as she caressed his face just as a mother who had not seen her child for a long period of time would when they were able to be together again.

"It is a trick," I screamed as loudly as I could. I was not sure if he could hear me. I had prepared him for Lucifer's tricks, knowing he would most likely resort to fake visions, as he had done to me up on the cliff. I had not contemplated that he might use Lumen's family as an illusion to try and distract him. I should have.

"Lumen," I screamed again. If he could hear me, he was not responding to my voice.

He stood face to face with the image of his deceased mother. After a long moment, Lumen stepped past the illusion and continued pull the wings from the tree. As he worked, he became surrounded by all six of his family members.

Lumen did not look to either side but continued to rip feathers from the tree. His mind was stronger than the illusions. The illusions moved in closer to him, obscuring his body from my sight. Then, with one swift motion, Lumen's brother reached out in front of him and grabbed Lumen's shoulder and pulled Lumen to the ground with so much force the ground shook.

Fighting back, Lumen struck his brother on the side of his face. When he did ,the flesh tore away, reveling scabby green skin.

My heart dropped as I realized that Lucifer had sunk even lower than I had ever believed. He was not using a vision or an illusion to distract Lumen; he'd cloaked members of his own army in the faces of Lumen's family.

I wondered how they were able to be on this planet. Lucifer was the only member of Hell that should have that ability before the seventh trumpet sounded.

Then I thought of the tree being rooted in Hell. Had Lucifer somehow torn the veil between Melahem and Hell?

What I did know for fact was that Lumen was being attacked by demons and there was a strong barrier that was preventing me from helping him. I had to help him somehow, but first I had to break down the barrier caused by the wings of the fallen angels.

I shoved my hands deep into the crust of the planet, pushing down hard until my arms were buried past my elbows. I closed my eyes and concentrated on every living being within Melahem that I could. I pulled energy from the plants, the infected water, the mutated animals, and the dying people of the city. I reached deep into the root system of the earth.

I could not push Lumen from my mind. My anger with Lucifer grew and I could feel the heat of my emotions rising. I fed that heat and I built upon it. I thought of all of the evil acts that Lucifer had committed over the millennia and how much pain he had caused. I focused on the vision of Lumen's family, crucified at the edge of the desert. I thought of the Waters' losing their newborn child to the smog filled air of Melahem. I thought of the potential that the humans had had at their creation and how they had squandered their gifts and pushed aside their blessings.

I let out a roar that I could not control. I bellowed in anger and I could feel flames shooting from my hand and through the ground. I opened my eyes and saw a crack running from through ground from where I stood all the way to the tree.

The wings burst into green and orange flames as they melted. I could not help but smile at the sight.

The wings flowed like thick tar down the tree. As the flames burnt out, I could feel the barrier slipping away.

Once there were no wings—not even a feather—left, I pulled my arms from the ground and ran to Lumen's side, where I was met with the demons that were masquerading as his family.

His sister and father stood before me, shoulder to shoulder, staring down at me. My body was exhausted from the successful effort to destroy the wings. I tried to gather whatever energy I had left, but it took too long. I looked up in time to see a fist crashing down. I dropped to my knees and rolled to my left. I pulled up my right leg and kicked my boot into the side of the knee of the demon that attempted to attack me. I pushed with all of the force that my body could muster. I heard a satisfying *crack* and saw where the demon's true skin broke through the mask that it was wearing. Its leg was covered in red boils and black blood trickled down its length.

I was able to muster enough energy together to knock the demon that looked like Lumen's sister onto her back.

As I regained my feet, one of the demons came up from behind me and, before I could move out of the way, I felt a large claw dig deep into my left shoulder. The demon hoisted me from the ground, and another claw dug into my right leg and lifted me so that I was hanging sideways.

I screamed in pain as I felt the claws tearing at my flesh. The demon swung me back and there was nothing that I could do to stop myself from being hurled at the tree. My body was too weak.

I could see it coming closer and closer.

I landed hard, then slid to the ground. The physical agony I felt was indescribable.

The trunk of the tree was still warm from the flames that had melted the wings. It was sticky like sap, oozing around the hard bark that lay beneath. Tiny purple and white lines ran through the bark. The tree was still surging with my energy.

I placed both of my hands on either side of my body, clutching the roots of the tree. I pulled the fragments of my power back and I could instantly feel my wounds healing.

I saw Lumen fighting with three of the monsters a hundred feet or so in front of me and sent out a shock through the ground, pushing it around Lumen and up the legs of Lucifer's soldiers.

They fell back and Lumen was able to obtain the higher ground. He grabbed a larger stone from the ground and dropped to the side of one of the demons. He began pounding the side of its skull.

I focused my attention on the other three who were walking towards us. They were grouped close enough together that I could concentrate on all three of them without hurting Lumen.

I hurled a larger amount of energy at them. Flames shot up from the ground and spread quickly over their flesh. Just because demons live amongst the flames does not mean that the bodies they inhabit cannot be destroyed by them.

The three danced around attempting to put the flames out as they shrieked. Soon it was just their nerves twitching and their bodies fell to the ground and the flames consumed their carcasses. A mist-like light came floating up around them. Slowly, their bodies dissipated as they were pulled back into Hell where they belonged.

There was no way to truly kill a demon—or any being, for that matter. All souls survive; it is only the physical that can be destroyed.

Once all the demon-possessed bodies were disposed of, either by Lumen and his rocks or me and my fire, Lumen did not pause to rest. He looked up at me and then at the tree. Raw energy began swirling around him.

His anger is the key. There was so much power in it, I knew, because he was not only kindling his own fury, that of the Creator as well.

Lucifer had created true chaos. He had cracked the city, and he had cracked Lumen, but in some cultures, before the last war, cracks in things were filled in with gold, making them stronger and more valuable, rather than broken. I prayed that Lumen's cracks would hold together through what was about to happen.

Lumen rose and began walking toward me. I pushed myself up from the ground as well and met him halfway. He did not speak. I could see the red flame flickering in his soul and in his eyes. He looked over my shoulder at the tree, then back at me again.

I knew he could destroy it now. I nodded, giving him my blessing. It was time to end the terror that the tree and Lucifer had brought to the city.

I had almost forgotten about the infected people that surrounded us. They had become a distant noise, a background that did not seem out of the ordinary any longer. People were still fighting and lighting buildings on fire, arguing over the existence of multiple planets, various gods, and what Melahem was like before the war. They were still exercising the special talents the fruit had unlocked within their minds, and some were still killing and eating their neighbors.

Then I noticed something that sent chills down my spine. Not one them was trying to keep us away from their beloved tree. I felt a pang of worry strike the pit of my stomach. Something was wrong.

I turned my attention back to Lumen, who had begun peeling pieces from the tree. It began to ooze black sap and soon Lumen's hands were covered in the sticky liquid.

Once he had peeled all of the bark from a large area in the middle of the tree, he balled his hands into tight fists and punched at the clear spot. He kept hitting, over and over, until his own blood was running down his arms.

As he punched, he screamed his rage, just as he had when we first saw his crucified family, the second time I had witnessed him freezing time with his anger.

As his roar echoed through the city of Melahem, I witnessed the phenomena once more. Everyone was frozen in place.

Lumen focused all of his anger on the tree. As he prepared to throw yet another punch, a purple spark shot from his fist. Energy began to flow around both of his hands. Large pieces began to fly off of the tree as he struck it. He carved a hole in the tree so large he could have crawled inside its trunk.

Lumen stopped his assault on the tree, stepped back, and examined his work. He walked back up to the tree and placed one hand on either side of the hole he had created. He began to push. He pushed until his arms began to shake. Energy coursed through his hands and up the trunk of the tree.

Purple energy ran up the tree, zig zagging around the bark like lightning bolts. The energy ran through the limbs of the tree to the leaves and the fruit, setting them on fire.

As Lumen continued to push, the tree started to crack. The bark split up the middle of the trunk. The ground shook as the roots of the tree began to snap and break through the ground, flinging gravel and dirt into the air.

Lumen screamed again, and the tree snapped in half. Each side fell, crashing to the ground. Flames shot from his hands, and Lumen ignited both halves of the tree at the same time. Black smoke billowed. The embers glowed green.

Lumen dropped his arms and fell to his knees. Time began to move again. The people of the city looked stunned, but at least they were not killing each other anymore, nor were they attempting to control powers that they were never meant to possess.

I walked over to Lumen, stepping over the broken ground where the tree had been uprooted, and knelt down in front of him. He was breathing deeply. I could see his chest rising and falling. I took his bloodied hands in mine. I used my own energy to heal his raw knuckles.

"Did ... it ... work?" Lumen asked between gulps of air.

"Yes."

A jagged smile crack across his face. He turned to the people of Melahem. It was obvious that the poison no longer had an effect on them.

I still felt uneasy. It should have been more difficult to get to the tree. Then I smelled it: vanilla and cherry blossoms. There was a large green dome just beyond the burning halves of the tree. Lucifer was standing to the side of the dome, and I could see something moving inside of it.

I stood to get a better view of what my brother was holding captive. As I stepped closer, I could tell that there were people trapped under his energy. I heard a cry. The voice was too shrill to be that of an adult. My heart sank.

"The children," I screamed.

I watched as a young toddler reached out and touched the side of the dome. The shock threw him backwards and he screamed in pain.

"No!" I exclaimed, charging toward Lucifer.

"You should have taken my offer, sister," he sneered.

Before I could reach him, he was gone, and so was the dome of children.

"How?" I whispered.

I fell to my knees, tears flowing down my face. I screamed in rage. My voice was met with the bellow of a trumpet.

THE THIRD TRUMPET

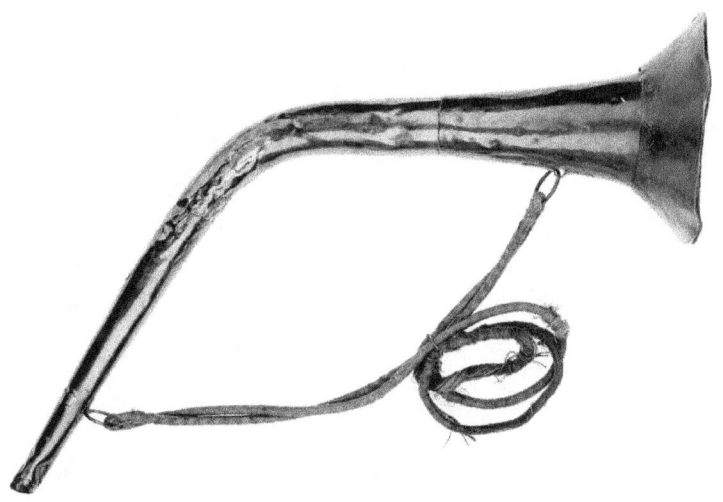

CHAPTER TEN

When the third trumpet sounded, the ground shook with a force much stronger than the it had with the first two. I looked in awe at the sky. It looked as though the sun was rising and coming closer to the Earth. For a moment, I truly believed that the sun was crashing down at us.

The air grew warmer by the second. The sky became brighter and brighter until I was blinded.

I struggled to breathe as the air grew thicker and hotter. I could feel sweat beading on the brow of my head and running past my ears.

A thunderous noise filled the air. It reminded me of the sound airplanes made back before the last war. It sounded and felt as though one was flying only inches above my head.

I did not know if this event was caused by the Creator or my brother.

I attempted to open my eyes, but they began to burn, so I squeezed them tight again. I heard something crash into the ground with such force it threw my body several feet back, even though I was already laying on the ground. I was paralyzed. I could hardly breathe. All of my senses were in overdrive and I could not calm them down. I could feel my body twitching as an unnatural energy coursed over and through me. I could feel sparks shooting out of the tips of my fingers, but I could not control it. I could not stop it.

My thoughts flew to Lumen. I wondered how this was impacting him. His human body was so much more susceptible to the elements than mine. I feared for his safety. But I still could not move to try to find him.

I forced myself to breath slowly. My mind raced. The image of Lucifer standing with the dome of green energy that he had trapped the children of the city in was burned into my mind. The scene with the poor child who had reached out and touched the dome, the energy tossing him backwards like a weightless rag, played over and over again in my head.

I feared what Lucifer might do to them—or for what he might have already done. They could not defend themselves against the devil. My brother had broken all of the rules of the reaping when he first came to Melahem and murdered Lumen's family. Now he had the children of the city. They were the ones I came to fight for. I prayed that their lost souls would be regained and that their Light would shine before the last trumpet bellowed though Melahem, before my brother was allotted his turn on Earth.

I did not understand how he was able to come to Earth and interfere with the reaping in the ways that he had. Something was wrong. The barriers between Earth and Hell had been broken. How else could he have planted the Tree of the Knowledge of Good and Evil right in the heart of the city? And his demons had come to Earth with apparent ease when he had sent them to fight and distract Lumen and me.

I was not yet sure how Lucifer had gotten away with what he did, but I promised myself I was going to find out. I had to. I had to find the children.

Where could he have taken them? Could he have taken them to Hell? How could this be allowed? Why was Lucifer being permitted to interfere with my reaping?

My mind whirled with questions I did not have the answer to

I took a deep breath and tried to slow my mind. I needed to take on my issues one step at a time. I could not help the children — or Lumen — if I could not help myself first. I concentrated on my heartbeat. It was racing. I breathed in deeply, so that I could feel my lungs inflating with air. Although it burned with the heat of the energy, I held the air in for ten seconds, and then let it out slowly. I repeated this pattern until I could feel my mind calming.

As my heart rate slowed, I was able to begin concentrating on my energy. My arms were out to my sides as I lay on the broken ground of the city. I forced my fingers down into the dirt. I wiggled them back and forth, digging down deeper, until they were buried.

I concentrated on the core of Earth. Molten lava swirled miles below; it was strong with energy. I could begin to feel a connection with it through the tiny layer of crust that I had broken through. I pulled the energy to me.

My fingers felt on fire as the energy began flowing through my body. I could feel the lava in my bloodstream. I could feel the blood flowing through my veins. I could feel my heart pumping blood to every corner of my body and every synapse firing in my brain. I was completely connected to every miracle that was happening inside of my body. I began to feel strong.

Next, I needed to focus on controlling my muscles. I started with my feet. I could feel the blood pumping though them. I flexed my toes and tapped them against the inner lining of my boots. From there I worked my way up.

I was finally able to push myself into a sitting position. Slowly, I opened my eyes. The blinding light had ceased. The city was illuminated with flames, and the tree's embers were still glowing.

I looked around at the city of Melahem. It was in ruins. As much as I wanted to rush to find the children Lucifer had stolen, I needed to get to Lumen first. I needed to make sure he had survived whatever it was that whited out the sky.

I forced myself up off the ground. My entire body was shaking. I steadied myself with the mounds of uprooted rock and dirt that surrounded me.

As I made my way around one half of the burning tree,I saw what had crashed into Melahem. It was a large comet, at least fifty feet in diameter, still burning bright with the heat that it had absorbed as it plummeted through the atmosphere.

Woodworm. I recognized what I was looking at. This was not a stray rock floating mindlessly through space that happened to find its way to this planet. This was a comet sent from the heavens, sent as a test. Woodworm would turn the groundwater of the planet stale. Anyone who drank the water would become bitter towards God as well as their neighbor.

One thing at a time, I reminded myself. I needed to make sure that Lumen was safe. I still felt unbalanced and walked with my hands out to my sides in an attempt to help steady myself. The ground beneath my feet was loose, which didn't help. With every step, I slipped and slid. Once I was able to make it around the second half of the tree, I saw Lumen.

He was lying flat in his back with his eyes closed. I could see the energy counting through his body. Small shocks, little purple lightning bolts, were shooting back and forth on his bare skin.

His body was convulsing from the energy, but he was not breathing.

I attempted to place my hand down on his chest to see if I could feel his heartbeat, but my hand was thrust away with a harsh jolt of electricity. I had forgotten that although I had gained control of my body, the foreign energy was still very much alive within me.

The jolt that shot my hand away also made Lumen's body jump. His chest rose and his body flopped hard as he landed back on the ground.

Whether his heart was beating or not when I first knelt by his side, I could visibly see that he was breathing now. The shock of my touch might have brought him back to life.

His mouth opened wide. He was gasping for air. I reached out to help him roll to his side, but I stopped myself just before I sent another harsh shock through his recovering body. I pulled in my arms and placed my hands on my knees.

"Roll on your side," I instructed. "It will be easier for you to breathe."

Lumen slowly rolled over onto his left side and pushed himself up on his forearm. His body was shaking. The muscles in his arms and legs twitched as he moved into a sitting position. I could tell that it was difficult for him.

"I cannot touch you without shocking you and causing you pain," I explained as I kept my distance.

Lumen breathed deeply and gave a harsh cough. He nodded to me in understanding.

It was hard for me to not to reach out and touch him, make sure he was all right. His human body was not meant to endure any of the events that had unfolded over the past night. I only hoped that the angelic power was strong enough in him for a full recovery.

He pushed himself up against a large mound of dirt that had been pulled up when he had destroyed the Tree of the Knowledge of Good and Evil. He let his head fall back against the earth and took in breaths that were deep enough that I could see his chest rising and falling.

While he rested and regained his strength, I looked around at the city. If I had not witnessed what had happened, I would have never believed that it was the same place that I had first visited only a few days prior.

The air was coated in thick green smoke from the burning tree. The comet, Woodworm, had crashed through many of the city's main living quarters. Buildings that were stacked over ten stories high served as home for the many of the city's people who did not reside on a farm or on the waterfront. Their apartments, their homes, were nothing but rubble. Broken stones, cloth, and pieces of handcrafted furniture lined the streets—or at least what was left of the streets.

The people of Melahem were scattered across the ground. I could see the same energy that had taken over my and Lumen's bodies pulsing over them as well. I knew that their weaker bodies were not going to be able to recover from the attack easily. I want to go to them and to help them, but I knew I could not.

The Source of All had sent the comet, knowing full well what the energy would do to the people of the city. I could not interfere with The Plan. Besides, they had written their own fates. I knew that many, if not all, of the people who lined the city had no innocence, no Light, left within them. They would have been for my brother to claim, if not now, then by the seventh trumpet's blow.

"You cannot drink the water from neither the city, nor the sea," I began explaining to Lumen. "The comet that that crashed in the distance, its name is Woodworm. It has turned all of the water on the planet bitter. If you drink the water now it will cause you to become bitter as well."

"What are the people of the city to drink?" asked Lumen.

"Rain water," I replied. "Any fresh water will be safe."

"It has not rained in Melahem for weeks," said Lumen. "They will all die before they get a chance to be saved."

"It will rain soon," I said. "Fresh water will be sent."

I hoped that my words were true. I needed to say them out loud as much to convince myself of Creator's kindness as I was attempting to convince Lumen.

Lumen pushed himself up on to his feet. He placed his hands on his hips as he looked around at the broken city, shaking his head in disgust. I pushed myself off the ground and stood next to him. The sight was not a pleasant one.

"Will they survive?" He motioned to all of the bodies lying motionless on the ground.

"I do not know," I answered him honestly.

I followed Lumen as he made his way towards the comet, stepping around bodies and large pieces of demolished buildings.

The air around us grew warmer as we approached. Its energy was still strong as it sat buried within the walls of the apartment building. We could only come to one hundred feet of the enormous rock. The heat that was radiating off of it was still far too strong.

Lumen and I stood looking up at our next puzzle.

"What should we do?" he asked.

"I am not sure just yet," I said. "I think, for now, all we can do is wait."

CHAPTER ELEVEN

We left the city. By the time we made it to the sea, we had regained our footing. It was refreshing to be able to walk with stability. The water was still blanketed with the corpses of rotting fish. They crashed into the shore with stomach-turning thuds as the bodies slammed into each other.

We walked toward the homes of Melahem's fishermen. I needed to get away from the comet, the tree, the people of the city, and the smell of rotting fish. I needed to think, to come up with a plan.

The home of Lumen's family looked just as it had the first time I had visited the site. I stood behind him as he pushed the door open. I was relieved that Lucifer had not destroyed Lumen's home along with his family.

I walked to the side table that stood next to the couch where I had seen Lumen's father and brother sharpening their work knives and grabbed a candle that was sitting in an old metal holder. It looked to be from before the last war. I conjured a flame and lit up the house.

Lumen's face showed his sadness. I could only imagine the pain he must have been feeling. This was the first time that he had visited his family home since before they'd all been crucified. He went from room to room, opening doors, looking inside. Being in the empty house made losing his family even more of a reality for Lumen. He had not had to face the reality of their deaths since we'd burned their bodies. Lumen had been able to use their deaths as a source of power, but the reality of them being gone had not fully settled in his mind. While Lumen took some much-needed time alone, I began looking around his house. The walls were mostly bare. A large fishing net hung on the ceiling in the sitting room, stretched so that it hung down about a foot. There were driftwood shelfs scattered around the room that were actually quite attractive. They were decorated with polished sea stones of varying colors that gave the sparsely furnished room a welcoming feeling. In the kitchen, the large dining table was still set with plates, forks, knives for all six members of Lumen's family. Each plate was filled with fruit that was still firm and had not begun to rot yet. I was pleased that Lumen would have something to eat. There was also a large serving plate waiting on the counter next to a bucket of fresh water. I assumed that they had been cooking a fish over the firepit when Lucifer had come for them.

I cautiously smelled the water in the bucket; it smelled only of the usual pollution. It did not carry the bitterness of Wormwood. Lumen would have enough drinking water to last him for a couple of days.

I heard a rustling sound coming from the back hallway and turned to see Lumen dressed in a clean set of clothes. His eyes were red from tears, but his features were composed.

"I have good news," I said, not wanting to dwell on his sorrow. "You have enough food and drinking water to last you for at least three days. This should be plenty of time to collect more untainted water."

Lumen nodded. "It looks like they were cooking dinner." He made sure to keep his face turned away from me as he investigated the scene in the kitchen.

"Yes."

Lumen picked up an apple-like fruit on the plate that was the closest to him. His Light flicked as he tightened his grasp on the fruit and juice began oozing from where his fingernails had pierced the skin.

"Lumen," I said quietly. I took a step towards him.

He took a deep breath, the fruit shaking in his hand. Small red sparks shot between his fingers. Lumen slammed the fruit back down onto the plate with such force that the clay dish cracked into pieces.

"Damn," Lumen cursed under his breath.

He began attempting to sweep the shattered pieces into his hand. Small shards of the plate broke through the skin of his hand. His blood was beginning to stain the table.

"Lumen," I whispered his name. I reached around him and pulled the nearest chair out from under the table. I leaned in closer, gently pushing him down so that he was sitting in the chair.

I pulled out another and sat next to him. I grabbed his bloodied hand in mine and pulled the sharp clay from his palm.

It did not take much of my energy to heal the small cuts and to stop the bleeding.

"Lucifer stole my family when they were sitting down to dinner," said Lumen in a shaky voice. "He stole them from me because of *me*." He put a strong emphasis on the last word.

"No," I told him. "This is not your fault. You are not to blame for any of it."

"Then who is?" Lumen growled. "You?"

"I am more to blame than you are," I said. "But this is all because of Lucifer. He is breaking the reaping code."

"He needs to be stopped."

"He will be." I hoped that my words would stand true. I had never had to battle my brother on this level before. I had a lot of thinking to do myself.

"You should rest," I said. I could see his exhaustion. His eyes had grown heavy and his words long.

"I don't want to rest," he snapped. "I want to stop Lucifer and help bring back my family."

Red light was brightly glowing throughout his entire body. His anger was rising as he sat and stared at his empty home. I did not blame him for his outburst of anger. All of the emotions he had been suppressing over the last couple of days were coming to the surface and he was being forced to accept the death of his family all over again.

"I will leave you to your thoughts," I said. I stood and started towards the door.

"Azrael," he called.

"You need time to collect your thoughts," I said, turning back to face him. "You need time to cope without it thinking that I am criticizing you over your emotions or believing that I am waiting for you to assist me in stopping my brother. You did not have enough time to to mourn their deaths, and I apologize for that."

At my words, his Light calmed to a dim white.

"I will be back before morning," I promised. "You really should eat and try to get some rest."

I walked outside into the night. I knew Lumen would be safe from my brother for the night. He would have used too much of his energy transporting the children to whatever hellish place he chose to come after us now. Lumen needed some time to himself, and I wanted to go back into the city and take a closer look at the comet.

I could feel a difference in the air as I approached the city. The energy had begun dispersing and was not as thick and difficult to move through as it had been, although a coating still remained. I could see a web sparking through the air and over the ground, all different hues of reds, purples, oranges, and blues.

With every step, I experienced a light shock spark through the bottom of my boot. I felt as though I was breathing in the sparks as well, and electricity filled my lungs. The energy moving through my veins felt tiny needles stabbing me everywhere.

I pushed through regardless. I needed to get closer to the comet if I was going to be able to help Lumen avoid becoming infected with Wormwood.

I could hear mumbles of voices in the distance. The people of the city had begun waking from their energy-induced comas. Three men and two women who looked to be around Lumen's age were pacing the ground in front of the comet. To my surprise, each one of them had a small spark of Light inside. Each was a different color. I have never seen such Light in the humans of Earth. I was unsure if their Lights were pure or only residue from the comet.

As I approached them, I was able to make out the words that they were speaking to each other.

"What is it?" asked a girl with long black hair.

"It looks like a stone," replied a man whose short dark hair that matched hers. "But what's this light around it?"

The Lights was drawing me to them. When I was about ten yards away, another girl, this one darker complected, with long hair the color of beach sand, looked directly at me.

They can see me. But their Lights are not pure.

"Who are you?" asked the girl. She took a step towards me as the other four turned to face me as well. Her eyes reminded me of the stormy eyes of Caleb Waters. I wondered briefly if she could have been related to the elderly couple.

"Are you all right?" she asked, walking towards me, breaking from the group. She stepped softly over broken pieces of concrete and uprooted dirt. As she approached me, I could see a glowing light in her eyes.

The light was unlike anything that I had seen in a human in all of my years of watching them.

It must be the energy from the comet. Maybe it has affected the humans similar to the way that the fruit from Lucifer's tree did.

The woman stopped an arm's distance away from me.

"Are you still sick from the fruit?" she asked.

She reached out a hand and cupped the side of my face with her fingers and palm. I felt myself flinch away from her. My reaction was purely reflexive; her actions caught me off guard. It was rare for a human to see me. This one not only could see me, but she was not frightened by my appearance, and she wished to make contact with me purely of her own free will.

"Your face is so pale," she said, looking me over, "and your eyes look as though you are still infected with the poison. You aren't acting like the others who ate the fruit, though. They were like wild beasts and tore the city apart."

"I am not infected," I said.

I took a step backwards, away from the woman. She dropped the hand she had been holding my face with down to her side. She looked to be as confused with the situation as I was.

"Oh," she said. "Sorry. It's just your eyes … and your veins."

Her eyes moved quickly, darting around my body as she looked me over once more. She reached up and touched the side of her own face, as though she was feeling for a difference within herself.

"Are you ready to go Home?" I asked. I believed I already knew the answer I was going to receive, but I thought my question would help me make sure my assumption about the comet's energy was correct.

"Home?" she asked. "All of our homes were either destroyed by the fires or by the people who were infected by the fruit. We have no homes to return to."

I was sad that her Light was not pure. I had been hoping I would be wrong and that I would be able to free their souls before dawn.

"Who are you?" she asked, looking me up and down yet again.

I waited a moment before answering. I looked behind her at the four other people standing huddled together, watching our interaction. They appeared frightened and perplexed by their situation.

"My name is Azreal," I said. "What are your names?"

"My name is Pax," she replied. "These are my brothers, Rex and Val." She pointed to two men who shared her darker complexion and blonde hair, although their eyes were nothing like hers. "And these are—were—our neighbors, Sage and Lajos." She gestured at the dark-haired woman and the man standing next to her.

Slowly, her companions began to make their way toward us, staying close together. I could see their fear flickering. Pax was different. She had no fear. Her Light was stronger than the others, even if it was only an effect of the comet. It was clear that she was the leader pack. I also assumed that she was the reason they had survived and managed to not fall victim to the fruit of the tree that plagued the city.

"This is Azrael," Pax introduced me.

The men all nodded in acknowledgment of her statement.

"Azrael," Sage repeated my name. "That's an interesting name. I haven't heard of it before."

"It is an old name," I explained.

"Did you see what happened to the city?" asked the man Pax had identified as her brother Val. "A flaming stone fell from the sky."

"Yes, I saw it."

"It destroyed the few buildings that were left of the city after all the fire and the people were through. There's nothing left," said Val. Sorrow washed over his face as he looked around at his surroundings.

"None of you have a safe place to sleep?" I asked.

They all looked exhausted. Their clothes were torn and stained. Their hair was full of dirt and dust, their faces were filthy, and their lips were visibly cracked and dry.

My stomach twisted as I thought of what might happen to them once the rest of the city came back to life. I was not sure how the energy from the comet would affect the rest of the residents.

"No," replied Pax. "Our homes were destroyed when the fire rained down on us. We watched everything we had burn to the ground. We're from the other side of the city. Our families were farmers, and the crops burned along with our possessions."

"I am sorry." I truly meant the words. It was always difficult to watch good people and families get torn apart during a reaping.

"Why is this happening to us?" asked Rex. He looked directly at me as though he knew I held the answer. "What have we done to deserve this?"

"I have a place that you can stay for the night," I said. It was not the proper time to explain the trumpets and the end of Melahem to the humans.

I did not believe that Lumen would mind if they shared his home for the night. He might even enjoy the company of other humans after only having me to speak to for so long. I also figured that since I could not sleep, I would be able to keep a watchful eye on our guests.

"You're serious?" asked Pax, her eyes wide with excitement. "You have a place where you'd let us stay?"

"I do," I assured her. "It is in the fishing village. You will be safe there for the night. Be sure to only drink the collected rainwater from the barrels, though; the sea and groundwater is not safe to drink."

They did not protest or ask questions. They followed me away from the comet and along the shoreline. I led them around the piles of fish carcasses and into the village. When we arrived at Lumen's home, I gently pushed the door open and lit a candle for the others to see where they were walking. I searched the cabinets of the kitchen until I was able to find cups to pass out water from a bucket on the counter.

"Thank you," said Pax. She quickly brought the cup to her lips and drank. I passed out the rest of the cups and the others followed suit, thanking me and gulping down the water.

"Stay here," I instructed them. "Someone is sleeping in the back bedroom, so please be mindful."

I conjured a small light and examined the hallway to the right of the sitting room. There were three doors, two to my left and one at the very end of the hall.

I was thankful to find that each one of them was a bedroom that had belonged to some member of Lumen's family. The beds were all made and, while there weren't enough for everyone to sleep alone, I assumed that doubling up for the night wouldn't be a problem.

"There are three beds, one in each room on this side of the hallway," I said, walking back to the sitting room and pointing to the right of the couch. "A couple of you will have to bunk together, but no one else will be staying there for the night."

"Thank you," exclaimed Pax.

She jumped up from the couch and wrapped her arms around me. It was an odd feeling, being embraced by a human. It was not something that happened often.

"Yes," said her brother Rex as he met her at my side. "Thank you for everything."

I heard a noise coming from the back of the house. There was a soft rustling sound before the bedroom door to the left of the couch swung open and Lumen stumbled out of the room. He was rubbing his eyes and looking around at all of the people standing in the middle of his home.

"What?" He looked at me. "Who are these people?"

"I'm Pax." She introduced herself before I had a chance to answer. Her voice was soft and appreciative. She stepped up to Lumen and shook his hand.

"These are my brothers, Val and Rex," she continued, "and these are our neighbors, Sage and Lajos."

Each nodded at Lumen as they were introduced.

"Hello," Lumen said, and came to stand beside me.

He placed his hand on the back of my arm and guided me out of the front door. I could not tell what he was feeling. His Light had been affected by the comet just as the others had been.

"These people can see you," he said, "like I can see you?"

"I do not know," I replied. "The energy from the comet had affected their Lights, much like Lucifer's fruit was affecting the people who ate it, but they can see me, yes."

"Where did they come from?"

"I found them when I went back into the city to look at the comet once more. I was curious to see how it affected the people of the city. I found out they did not have anywhere safe to spend the night, so I brought them here. They can sleep in three bedrooms down the hall. I am still unsure how the other people of the city will react to the energy once they wake up—if they wake up—and didn't want to risk their safety. Besides, I thought that you would not mind a little company. You can speak with them about everything that has happened to you. They have seen the destruction of the trumpets and they can see me."

"They'll think I'm insane, or infected with the fruit, if I talk about you and what's happening to Melahem," replied Lumen.

"No," I stated, "they will not."

"How do you know that?" His voice was rising.

"Because you will convince them. They will see what we can both do, they will hear your stories, and they will believe. I do not know if their Lights are pure, but speaking to you could ensure their survival of this planet's reaping. You could save them."

Lumen shook his head and ran his fingers though his hair. I could tell that he was still exhausted. His mind must have been spinning as he tried to comprehend everything that was happening.

"There are two other bedrooms on the side of the house that my room is on," Lumen said. "They can use them as well. That way, no one will have to share a bed."

"Thank you."

Lumen did not reply. He brushed past me and pulled the door to his home open. As we arrived back in the sitting room, five pairs of eyes settled on us.

"There are two other bedrooms on this side of the house," said Lumen, as he pointed to the hallway on the left. "You won't have to share beds. You're welcome to stay for as long as you need."

"Thank you," said Val.

Each of them rose and went to Lumen to either wrap their arms around his neck or to shake his hand. I could see their appreciation of his generosity painted on their faces.

"I'm sorry that I don't have more to offer, but feel free to help yourselves to whatever there is," Lumen said, his voice sounding exhausted.

He stretched and scratched the back of his head as he turned to look at me. His face had lightened slightly.

"I could not leave them out there to die," I whispered to him as he came closer to me.

"I know," he said sincerely. "And you're right, it will be nice to have other people to talk to about everything that's going on. We can share our stories—and maybe we can save them, and others."

"Exactly," I agreed.

A small smile cracked across Lumen's face. He was willing to do everything in his power to help me and to work to bring his family back. He had a lot power on his own, but I had learned that many times humans are stronger when they work together. I had the idea that maybe with some help Lumen and I would be able create a small army of innocents to stand up against my brother.

CHAPTER TWELVE

I sat at the kitchen table as the five stray humans and Lumen slept. The night was calm. I could hear all six of them softly breathing as they fell into a deep sleep that I knew would last past sunrise. They were all exhausted and they had not settled in to rest until the middle of the night.

Quietly, I made my way outside to the fruit tree that stood, past its season, barren. A cool wind blew in from the sea. Although it carried the stench of dead fish, it was still a welcomed breeze. The heat from the comet lingered, adding to the already warm night

I placed both of my hands on the roots of the tree and willed it to bear fruit. Our guests had eaten everything in the kitchen, so I knew they'd need more sustenance in the morning. I suspected they'd want to return to the city to search for others like themselves.

As I plucked the fruit from the tree, I felt an unnatural connection to the humans. I've never denied that I have never been fond of the species, aside from the children—and, more recently, Lumen. I'd found him to be a pleasant companion; perhaps the other five could be as well.

A rush of hope mixed worry rained down on me as I whispered a prayer that the newcomers would still be able to see me in the morning, that their Light swould not fade away. If they did I had little hope of saving more of the people of Melahem.

My anger rose as my thoughts returned to the dome of children Lucifer had captured. The image continued to haunt me. I tried to think of any and every place that he might have taken them.

I took a breath and forced the memory from my mind. I hugged the fruits to my chest and walked back towards the house. I pushed the door open with my back and shoulder and gently set the fruit down on the kitchen table, dividing them two per chair. All six of the humans would have a decent breakfast.

I went back outside and watched as the haze began to lift around the sea and the sky lightened. I could still feel the energy from the comet pulsing through the air. I could taste it. If the humans were going to survive, they were going to need rainwater to collect, and soon.

I watched as the grey sky continued to brighten, wondering what the new day would bring. There was certain to be confusion in the city as people realized there was essentially no city left to live in.

Footsteps landed softly on the wooden floor of the house. I turned and went back inside, surprised to see Lumen standing in the middle of the sitting room. I had expected him to sleep much longer. He yawned as he began stretching his arms and back.

"You look rested," I observed as I noticed that his Light had gone back to its soft white glow.

"I feel it," he replied.

As he approached me, I noticed that all of his wounds from the battle earlier were completely healed. He was moving fluidly and did not seem to be in any pain.

"I am glad that you are feeling well," I said. "You should eat and keep your energy up."

I motioned to the plate of fruit I had placed on the table. Lumen nodded in agreement and sat next to me.

"I need you to know there is a good chance that the others may not be able to see me when they wake," I said. "I suspect their ability to do so might have only been a result of the energy from the comet. If my hunch is correct, it will be up to you to help them see the truth. I will not be able to assist you; I cannot interfere in that manner."

"You truly believe that I have the power to save them," asked Lumen, "and the other people of the city?"

"I do," I told him. "I still believe you may even be able to save your family."

Footsteps echoed down the hallway to the right of the sitting room. We watched as Pax emerged into the hazy light of the morning. As I looked into her, I saw there was still a faint white Light within. It was nowhere near as strong as it was when I had first met her, but it was still there.

"Good morning," she greeted us.

Pax looked directly at me. She could still see me. I felt a smile break across my face.

"Breakfast," I said as I caught her eyeing the fruit. "Help yourself."

As she ate, her eyes seemed to brighten. I found myself staring at her irises. She reminded me so much of Caleb Waters. It was almost haunting to have her sitting next to me.

Soon, the others began to wake and join us. Val was the next person to enter the kitchen. When I looked into him, his Light had completely faded. His ability to see me had fully relied on the energy he had absorbed from the comet.

"Hey, more fruit." He smiled at Lumen and Pax. "Where is Azrael?"

"What are you talking about?" asked Pax, pointing at me "She's right here."

"He cannot see me," I said to Lumen. "His Light is gone."

"What?" Val scrunched up his face in confusion.

"Don't worry about it," said Lumen. "I've got a lot to explain to all of you, but it'll be easier if I wait until everyone's here."

Pax looked at me and I placed my hand over hers.

"Do not worry," I instructed her. "It will all make sense soon."

As the other three humans came into the kitchen and were unable to see me, I could see Pax's rising frustration and confusion rising.

"Will you please tell me what is going on?" she said to Lumen. "And why it is that you and I are the only ones who can see Azrael?"

"Because you and I are the only ones with pure innocence," Lumen said. "Azrael is an angel, and the only reason everyone else could see her was because of the energy that was radiating off of the comet. The energy came from the Creator, and that's how it could fill you with the power to see her."

They all looked at Lumen in disbelief.

"Is this true?" Pax asked, looking directly at me.

"It is," I affirmed Lumen's statement. "Everything he is about to tell you is the truth."

Pax took a deep breath and nodded.

"Okay." She sighed as she turned her attention back to Lumen. "Tell us everything."

I listened as Lumen recited our story. He told them of our trip into the desert. He spoke of the wolf-like creatures that had stalked us in the night and how I had pulled a fruit tree and a water spring from the ground. He explained how Earth was truly coming to an end and that Melahem was paying for the sins of the entire human race. When he began talking about Caleb and Viola Waters, Pax's face brightened.

"Caleb and Viola Waters?" she chimed in. "You met them?"

"Yes," replied Lumen. "Do you know them?"

"They are my aunt and uncle," she said excitedly. "My father and Caleb are brothers."

I smiled as my assumption that Pax was related to Caleb was confirmed. It also helped explain why she was still filled with innocent Light. I was curious about her brothers, though; they did not seem to share her blessings.

"Your uncle was a good man," I said, placing a hand on Pax's arm. "And your Aunt Viola was a true angel."

"Was? Have they passed away?"

"Azrael saved them from seeing the end of Melahem, just as she did with the child I told you about," said Lumen, jumping to my defense. "She sent them Home."

Pax pulled her arm out from under my hand and looked at me in shock. I could see her Light flickering red with anger.

"I'm sorry," she said to Lumen. "I need a minute alone."

Her brothers followed her outside. Lumen looked to me for an answer.

"You must let her grieve," I explained to him. "Give her a moment and then meet her outside. Explain to her everything that happened and how they had anticipated our arrival."

"Shouldn't you speak with her?" Lumen asked.

"No, you are the one who has to win them over," I said. "I cannot interfere."

Lumen gave a deep sigh, but nodded his understanding. He pushed himself away from the table and went into the yard where Pax was sitting with her brothers beneath the fruit tree.

"How was she able to harvest fruit from this tree?" asked Rex. "It's months out of season."

"Magic," Lumen answered.

"Magic?" Rex asked in an accusing tone. "So you are both witches."

The muscles in Lumen's face tightened at Rex's words.

"Here," he said, "let me show you."

Lumen dug his hand into the dirt around the tree and placed his thumb upon its root. He closed his eyes and concentrated, forging a connection with the tree. Small sparks of electricity shot off of his body as the tree began to glow. A low hanging branch just above where Pax and her brothers were sitting began producing fruit.

They jumped up at the sight. Pax covered her mouth in astonishment as she watched the tree grow new leaves and flowers before producing even more fruit.

Lumen pulled his hand from the ground. When he did, he drew a significant amount of energy up with it. He used the energy to form a large flame in his hands. He walked over to the firepit to the left of the tree and lit the driftwood inside.

"It is all connected," Lumen began. "The plants, the animals in the desert, the sea, us. We are all connected by energy. By life."

Lumen looked to me as he extinguished the flame in his hand, his face silently asking for my approval of the way he had explained magic. I nodded to him and smiled. I was proud that he had truly been listening to everything I had been teaching him and that he was now able to control his own abilities.

"How did you do that?" gasped Pax.

She reached out and grabbed Lumen's hands and inspected them, I assumed, for burn marks from the flames.

"This is sorcery," snapped Rex. "This is nothing but a trick."

"Magic," Lumen said to Pax, ignoring her brother.

"Magic?" She stared at him as though she thought him insane.

"It is real," he continued. "Everything I've explained to you is true."

Pax knelt at the base of the tree where Lumen had buried his hand in the. She dug her own hand in in the same place. She closed her eyes and ran her hand down the roots of the tree.

"Why can't I feel anything?" she asked.

"Maybe you don't know what you're feeling for. You have to concentrate on the energy," Lumen said.

He went to Caleb's niece and placed his hand over hers. He plunged her hand into the ground in the same manner I had once done to him, and used his own power to draw energy from the earth so that Pax could better understand. She needed to experience the power of the universe, of faith, firsthand in order for her to believe what he told her.

The door opened behind me and Sage and Lajos emerged from the house. I assumed that they could hear the conversation Pax was having with Lumen and that they were able to witness the flames that erupted from Lumen's hands.

Pax laughed as the energy ran up her arms and swirled around her. She watched the sparkling white and purple energy bolts shooting through the air around them. When Lumen let go of Pax's hand, the energy disappeared from their view. Pax held her hands out in front of her face and examined them carefully.

"I feel like a child," she said. She had a look of amazement plastered on her face.

"That is the point," I said.

"We should all strive to live with the innocence of a child," Lumen finished my thought for me.

I nodded, then I took Lumen aside to speak to him privately.

"I will be back soon," I said. "I am going to see what is going on in the city. You need to finish explaining everything that you know to the others."

Before I left, I observed the five newcomers examine the fruit Lumen had produced from the tree. The men circled the fire and held their hands up to the flames to see if they were real. Even with Rex's accusation of witchcraft, I witnessed as a small Light began to flicker in each of them. I knew that none of them, besides Pax, could see me yet, but I smiled. I knew Lumen would be able to win them over. He was a true fisherman.

CHAPTER THIRTEEN

Once in the city, I walked past the comet and the rubble and made my way to the last place I had seen my brother with his child prisoners. I crouched down and felt the ground where the dome had been.

Nothing. Lucifer had not left a trace of his energy behind. I was standing on nothing more than a patch of broken ground that looked the same as the rest of the city of Malahem, without any clue as to where to look for the children.

I felt defeated as I stood and turned towards the comet, the gift of the third trumpet. The energy it had carried though the heavens had dissipated. It appeared to be nothing more than a virus-carrying stone now.

Bodies still lined the pebble streets of the city. I could not tell from a distance weather any of them were still breathing, or if their life had been stolen from them over the last few hours.

There was no energy force pushing me away from Woodworm now. I was able to walk up to the stone with ease. It truly was enormous. If it was removed from the ground, it would leave a large lake-sized crater.

I expected to feel small sparks or some leftover residual energy from its journey when I touched it, but I felt nothing beyond the cold of the night air held in its porous structure. The rock was rough and covered with large holes. I lifted my foot up about six inches off of the ground and wiggled my boot into one, and, reaching my hands above my head, I found purchase on its ridges.

I slowly climbed up the large structure, carefully placing my hands and feet, for at least twenty meters. It was a little easier to breathe once I was standing on the top. I must have been standing just above the lower blanket of smog that covered the city.

Melahem looked as though it had just been through a war, rather than being the product of war's survivors. There was no building left in the city that was not missing a piece of its roof or an entire side of its structure. Each apartment complex and market building that was not complete rubble needed only another trumpet's bellow to shake the ground before they would come tumbling down as well.

There were more bodies than I had first realized, lining what used to be the streets of the city. They were laying amongst their burned belongings and rotting fruit from Lucifer's tree. The sight was disturbing.

I turned and looked out toward the water. It was a never-ending graveyard of ocean life. The volcano still stood in the middle of the sea.

It was no longer spewing hot lava and flames into the sky, but I had no doubt that it could easily become active once again.

The desert was also visible from where I was standing. I could see the cliff where I had spoken to my brother, when he had tricked my mind in to thinking that I was dying. I could see the mountains in the far distance and wondered what lay beyond them.

What else is out there?

A part of me wanted to teleport out past the mountains and see for myself, just out of pure curiosity.

Are there more people living over there? I did not think it likely; I would have felt them.

I enjoyed a few more deep breaths of the fresher air before making my way back down to the street. There was a young woman laying against a side of a half-burned couch. Her eyes were open and she seemed to be looking directly at me. There was no Light within her, though.

I knelt at her side. She was young, younger than Lumen and the other five humans, seeming to be in her teenage years. I placed a hand on the side of her neck to feel for a pulse, but I already knew before I outstretched my arm that there was no life. I closed the girl's eyes and bowed my head in sorrow and disappointment in the human race.

I scanned the rest of the bodies that littered the area. Not a single one of them showed any sign of life.

I used my abilities to gently lift all of the bodies, one by one, and float them over to the comet. Even if the people of the city had all died without any Light within them, they still deserved to have their bodies disposed of in a respectful manner. Besides, it was a sight I did not wish Lumen to witness. No one needed to see their city lined with the carcasses of their deceased neighbors.

I felt a small pang of sorrow that the people laying before me had not had a chance to talk to Lumen. Perhaps if they were able to hold on only a few hours longer, their fates could have been different.

I sighed and conjured a large blue flame in my hands. I walked to each body, lighting them first at their feet, and then walking around and setting their heads aflame.

The smell of such a large amount of burning flesh made my stomach turn, but I stayed with the bodies. I would not leave them until the flame burnt out. It did not take long before nothing was left except a pile of ash. They had not sparkled on their way to the heavens.

I knew where each of them had gone. They would be soldiers, fighting alongside my brother.

There was nothing more that I could do in the city without Lumen. The humans had written their own fate, and they needed a human to save them from it.

As I approached the fishing village, I noticed a large crowd of people standing on Lumen's property. As I got closer, I could see there were roughly twenty of them huddled around a large cauldron that was bubbling over the firepit. I was taken aback to see so many people with Lumen, and astonished to see that almost every one of them had a flicker of Light glowing within.

Lumen broke away from the crowd and hurried to me, smiling broadly.

"They saw my magic," Lumen exclaimed, his eyes shining with happiness.

"All of them?"

"Most of them. They're my neighbors," he explained, "and they saw what I did with Pax, when we pulled the energy from the tree and when I lit the fire pit with the flames I conjured. They all came over and listened to my stories about everything that's happened and what's going to happen. They all believe me, and most of them believe in you."

I smiled at Lumen's words. I knew he was telling the truth; I could see the villagers' Lights growing.

"They're all donating different vegetables, fish, and fresh water. We're making a stew for everyone to share," said Lumen. His voice was childlike and filled with delight.

"That is incredible," I replied. I rested a hand on Lumen's shoulder and looked at the good work he had done. "I am glad that you have won them over," I said. "Unfortunately, most of the people in the city did not survive the impact of the comet."

"Come and see," said Lumen.

I assumed he was too excited to have heard my last words. I did not argue with him. I followed Lumen into the crowd and observed as the neighbors all worked together to make a stew. It was incredible to watch the humans work with each other to accomplish a task. They were helping one another and sharing what they had. This was what Creator had in mind for the humans from the beginning of their creation. They were meant to be generous and kind.

Each one of them was contributing in some way to the process. Some were cutting vegetables. Others were donating the rainwater they had left over from before the comet. Some were cutting fish and adding the meat to the large cauldron as it bubbled over the fire. Everyone was helping.

Once the meat was safely boiled and the vegetables were soft in the stew, they began portioning out bowls of the cauldron's contents. I followed Lumen as he brought his inside and sat at the kitchen table with Pax and her brothers, who were already eating. As he walked past me, I caught a bitter aroma coming from the bowl before as he made his way past me.

Wormwood! The thought screamed in my mind. *Someone added infected water to the stew.*

"Lumen, no," I shouted. My heart dropped as I watched Lumen spoon the soup into his mouth. His Light changed as soon as it hit his tongue, dimming and fading to a dark blue that remined me of the night sky at twilight.

I felt myself slipping away from his reality. I felt a sense of desolation as he looked in my direction. He looked right through me, just like every other person in Melahem. He could no longer see me.

I felt a sinking feeling in the pit of my stomach as I realized just how alone I really was now. I knew that I always had the Almighty with me, but I was now physically alone on the planet. I had grown fond of having a companion. It was nice having a person to talk to.

There had always been a lingering thought in the back of my mind that would occasionally nag at me, reminding me that there was the very real chance of losing Lumen. I had always associated Lucifer with that potential loss, not a careless oversight.

I stood for only another moment, watching as he spooned a few more mouthfuls of soup from the bowl. He would grow bitter now, not only toward me, but toward everyone and everything that he would come into contact with. The Woodworm would slowly gnaw away at his soul.

All I could do now was pray for his Light to return. I believed that not only his life, but the lives of everyone in Melahem, depended on it.

I went out the door of Lumen's slightly off-kilter house and made my way to the water.

CHAPTER FOURTEEN

The scent of vanilla and cherry blossoms filled the air. The aroma made my stomach turn and my anger rise. My face tightened and I clenched my teeth together. My breathing became heavy as my mind raced with everything that I wanted to say to my brother.

I wanted to scream at him. I wanted to force him to tell me where he had hidden the children. I wanted to curse him for his actions.

I could feel Lucifer's breath on the back of my neck. I balled my hands into fists and screamed as I twisted my body. I swung my fist with all of my power directly at my brother's jaw—and it was blocked only millimeters away from Lucifer's face. I was not permitted to cause physical injury to my brother, just as he was not permitted to do so to me. Some power between angelic twins forbade it. I did not appreciate the fact that I shared blood with the monster standing before me.

Lucifer stoodwith his hands behind his back and a thin smile on his face.

"It is nice to see you as well, sister," he said. His voice was calm and cordial.

I had so much that I wanted to say, so many questions I wanted to force my brother to answer, yet I could not formulate the words. I could not even force my mouth open in an attempt to speak.

"How is your pet?" asked Lucifer.

I did not answer. I still could not speak through my rage.

"It looks as though Melahem has seen better days," he continued. "Your precious Earth has fallen to shambles."

"Where are they?" I growled, finally able to spew a few words.

"Whom are you referring to, sister?" Lucifer teased. "There are many theys in the universe."

I could feel my heart rate rising again. It was difficult to breathe.

"The children," I shouted, clenching my fists so tightly my fingernails drew blood.

"The children?" Lucifer echoed my words. His voice was calm. "They are safe."

"What have you done with them," I screamed, my temper inching out of control.

"You should have taken my offer, sister," Lucifer sneered. "I am still willing to negotiate a trade."

"Their souls are not for you to play with," I said. "Let me remind you that you have overstepped the boundaries of this reaping. It is not your time to be on this planet."

"Well, I do believe that if you were correct, some power would have prevented me from doing what I have done," he said.

He was right. No one had tried to stop him except me.

Questions and doubt swirled around in my mind. *How was it that Lucifer had not been prevented from stealing the children? And if Lucifer could interfere with the reaping, could I interfere as well?*

My mind stuck on that last question. *Does he want me to interfere?* Creator had always held onto the idea that there was still hope for the people of Earth, never truly giving up on them. Even now, at the end, there was Lumen with his powers as one last hope. But maybe not the last hope. Maybe *I* was supposed to save the planet.

"What are you thinking, dear sister?" Lucifer interrupted my revelation. "Please enlighten me."

"I was just thinking that you are right, brother," I replied, my tone even and thoughtful. "No one has tried to stop you."

And no one will try to stop me, I finished the sentence in my mind.

"Would you like to reconsider the trade?" asked Lucifer. The look of superiority on his face made me want to gag.

"No," I said plainly, to his obvious disappointment. "Now, brother, I am quite busy."

I did not feel the need to converse with him any longer. I did not need to get any information from him, neither about the children nor how he was interfering in my work. I had come to the realization that I could take the fate of Melahem into my own hands, and I was going to begin with saving its lost children.

"Well, until the next time, sister," he said, keeping a thin smile on his face. He took a step backwards and was gone leaving behind only a cloud of smoke and a few burning embers on the sand.

I can save the children. I smiled as the thought ran through my head. I did not need Lucifer's deal. I could save them on my own. The fact that it had taken me so long to come to this realization was frustrating, but I consoled myself by remembering that everything happens in its own time.

I needed to find a place to concentrate, away from Melahem, away from the bitter townspeople, and away from Lumen. I had instructed him to not drink the city's water, and it both angered and saddened me that he had forgotten to be cautious.

I walked the edge of the sea until I found a peaceful spot not covered in the carcasses of rotting fish. An old oak tree stood tall and strong a few yards from the shore.

I touched its trunk, closed my eyes, and connected my energy to its. Trees are wise and carry with them memories of all that they have seen.

Visions flashed before my eyes. I saw the war. I was standing right in the middle of everything. The streets were backed up with cars lined up bumper to bumper, their doors flung wide open. The people who had owned them had abandoned them and the rest of their possessions in the streets and ran screaming past me. They were running away from the sea.

I looked toward the ocean. Oversized metal ships were crashing to the shore, running through the shallow waters and onto the beach. They would never be able to get their ships back in the water, but no one else was going to be able to attempt to flee by sea.

The sound of the ships grinding against the ground and each other sent chills down my spine. They had run the ships so close together that their steel sides were scraping.

Men, women, and children were firing guns and homemade weapons in any, and every, direction both from the land and the boats.

A low roaring sound, much like the comet had made as it flew low over my head just before it had crashed into Melahem, drew my attention skyward.

The sky was blanketed in airplanes for as far as I could see. Small aircraft shot at each other and at the people on the ground until they parted and made room for five larger planes. I realized what they were carrying only seconds before the large bombs fell. The explosions were deafening. Although it was no more than a vision, I clutched the tree; it had somehow survived the bombing and would keep me safe.

When I dared to look around, nothing was left alive except for two-thirds of the tree and myself. The ground covered with blood, dead bodies, and metal shards.

I was preparing to let go of the tree and examine my surroundings when I was quickly thrust into a different vision. I had almost forgotten that I was witnessing the memories of the tree. If I had lost touch with it, I would once again be sitting alone at the edge of Melahem.

The next vision was much more pleasant. I was standing in the middle of a vast, lush forest, surrounded by tall ferns and colorful flowers. There were pine trees and tall maple trees that shielded me from the full heat of the sun. Small rays of sunlight filtered through the thick canopy of leaves. It looked heavenly as it streaked across the forest floor.

The oak tree that I was connected to felt different here. I quickly discovered the reason: the tree's trunk was only about six inches in diameter rather than the thirty or forty inches that it was in Melahem. The tree was showing me its earlier days, back when the forest was young. There was no way fpr ,e to tell how far back in time we had traveled, but it was obviously many years before the creation of

Melahem.

I inched my hand down the tree's roots. I settled my back against its trunk and felt the ground with my free hand. I could feel the richness in the soil. The lush green grass and mosses were soft to the touch as I ran my hand over the untainted vegetation.

Although I was only sitting in a memory, it was a strong one. The tree was older than Melahem, was older than the destruction of Earth. Power surged through it, even as it fought for life on the outskirts of the polluted city.

I dug my hand deep down into the soil of the forest floor. I closed my eyes and concentrated on the nature that surrounded me. I listened to the songbirds and the gentle sound of the ocean waves in the distance. I allowed the purity of the environment to fill me with its energy and peace.

CHAPTER FIFTEEN

I let go of the tree and the visions were lost.

I took a deep breath and let it out slowly as I began concentrating on the lost children of Melahem. Although the thought of them trapped under his dome made my stomach queasy, I had to concentrate on it. I had to focus on the children if I had any chance of finding them.

The first place I thought to look, of course, was Lucifer's very own domain. I hoped against hope that my brother did not take souls that were not his claim down into the pits of despaire that he called home. I connected myself with the fiery gates, but I did not sense the children there. I did not sense anything there. I felt nothing.

It must be another trick. Lucifer must have known that I would search for the children here first.

I pulled my thoughts away from Hell and began concentrating only on the children. *Where would Lucifer hide them?* I did not believe that he would injure his captives, not when he knew how much they had meant to me. He would use them to manipulate me in any way that he could.

I also did not think he would hide them on what was left of Earth. It would be too easy for me to feel their energy. So I began searching other nearby planets. Not many of them were able to support any kind of life, although they did have their reasons for existing in this particular solar system.

I searched deeper, past Earth's galaxy. I passed planets that I had not visited in years. There were star constellations and colorful suns that the people of Earth could have only dreamed of seeing. It was beautiful.

Then, as I searched just past the seventh planet of the Ruin Galaxy to the furthest planet from the Toran Sun, I felt them. I felt the children crying out in the darkness. Lucifer truly was playing with me. He had transported the children to my favorite planet: Corton.

I knew that I had people to help back in Melahem. I had to help Lumen come back to his senses and regain control of his mind, but he was safe for now, and I was not sure what condition the children were in. I had to get to Corton.

I closed my eyes and concentrated on the planet. It is not difficult for angels to teleport from one planet to the next, but it does take an extreme amount of concentration. I pictured the fields of Corton. The planet was covered in beautiful purple and pink flowers.

I could feel as my body left Melahem. It is an odd sensation, teleporting. When it happens, every particle of my being is broken down. My body was no longer a solid mass as I began traveling through space. I floated shapelessly until I found my destination. I could not see anything, space, or the lack thereof, as I was moving. I could only see what I was picturing in my mind. I was never as strong at teleporting as my brother was. It did not seem to consume as much of his energy as it did whenever I traveled from place to place.

When I was close to my destination, I could feel I was where I wanted to be. Once I arrived, I the molecules of my body fused back together, bit by bit. It was almost like being reborn. I could feel portions of my body that I could not feel when I was whole. I could feel everything working inside of my body. I could feel my liver filtering toxins, and the tiny bronchi of my lungs filling with air.

Once I was put together again, I saw that I was indeed at my destination. I was standing in the pure, warm light of two of the three moons of Corton. The fact that I had been indeed able to teleport to Corton could only mean that I was correct in assuming I was supposed to interfere on Melahem. If Creator did not want me to fight for the humans, I never would have been allowed to abandon the city and search for the children.

I began by walking along a large river. The air was fresh on Corton. There was no pollution. The only scents that I could smell were natural and pure: the blooming flowers of their large fruit trees and the sweet aroma of the river. The water on Corton always tasted like it was infused with honey.

The Cortonians were not industrial people. They lived simply, hunting, fishing, and gathering only what they needed to survive. They did not indulge in greed, or gluttony; they worked together. The people of Corton very much reminded me of the Native Americans of old Earth.

I bent down and cupped my hands in the water of the river, bringing the sweet liquid up to my lips. The sweet flavor stuck to the sides of my cheeks as I scooped another mouthful of water. It felt cool and smooth as it ran down the back of my throat.

The water on Corton was much thicker than the water of Earth, heavier and more nourishing. Drinking water from the river could cure the pains of hunger.

I could feel my body recovering from my long trip as the water reenergized my body.

As I continued on my way, I felt a presence watching me. Slowly, I turned my head and discovered that someone was standing nearby. Out of the corner of my eye, I could see a shadowy figure standing behind me to my left. I breathed a sigh of relief when I was able to be certain that it was not my brother lurking.

I laughed out loud as the tall bird walked out into the light of the two moons and I realized it was not a person after all. Standing six feet high with large eyes as white as the stars, the Snype would have been mistaken for a monster by the humans of Earth because of its coloring and skeletal figure, but I thought it was beautiful.

The closer it came, the more prominent the halo-like glow surrounding it became. It looked as though a living galaxy was walking toward me. A comforting feeling calmed my mind with every step that the animal took in my direction.

A strong wind blew off the river and the smell of rosehips filled the air. It was then that I realized that the Snype that was standing before me was not a creature of Corton at all. It was Creator with me in the darkness of the planet. It was something that I should not have required reminding of, but it was comforting all in the same.

"I need to save the children," I said to the magical creature.

The Snype gave a call that echoed through the night. My eyes locked with its for only a moment before it started walking away, leaving a glowing trail that made it easy to follow.

I took a deep breath and followed my guide through the thick forest of Corton, listening to the sounds of all of the creatures that depended on the darkness of the planet. Everything about Corton was slightly haunting. It was a planet fit for ghosts and semi-dark magic. I loved it.

The trees were purple, with leaves of such a deep shade that they looked black. The flowers had large lavender petals with bright pink veins running through them.

When the branches of the trees moved in the steady river breeze, it sounded as if they were whispering to each other. Maybe they were. I did know that the people of Corton had a great respect for nature, and especially for trees.

After a few minutes, I heard a low, hissing growl. I looked to my right and saw three sets of eyes staring at me. As they got closer, I could make out the figures to be those of large cats. There was an entire pack of them. I watched as one crouched down, ready to lunge, but as long as I stayed close to the Snype, they did not advance.

It was a unique feeling, being in the presence of my Parent, one that I never tired of. No two encounters were ever the same; I never knew what form I would encounter, male, female, or, as today, beast.

At the edge of the forest, I could see rows of torches burning and huts circling a large bonfire that sent blue sparks out into the night sky.

I could hear people speaking in an ancient Cortonian language, Pridice. Unlike most languages spoken on Earth throughout the centuries, Pridice was more flowing and free form. It was like a river of soft sounds that rolled off of the tongueIt was a language that was only spoken by the elders of the planet. They were strict in their practices, living on the outskirts of the main town to ensure they would not become tainted with the ideas of unknowing minds.

When we had made it to the first row of torches, we were met by a man I recognized from years ago. He was one of the youngest elders at the age of only two hundred and twenty-three.

His face was almost as pale as mine, and his eyes glowed in the light of the two moons. Small, intricately detailed tattoos covered his nearly naked body. They symbolized strength, knowledge, and age.

His eyes met mine and he swiftly bowed down before the glowing bird. I was sure that he had seen us approaching his home before we had exited the thick cover of the trees. When he straightened, I could see that his face was stern.

"Your brother has been through here," he said in Pridice.

"My apologies," I replied in his language. "Has he caused you any damage?"

"Not much," he said. "Come, my father would like to speak with you."

I followed the elder past the blue torches and huts to the middle of the site. Sitting on a woven blanket beside the large blue fire was Rege, the eldest of all of the Cortonians.

Rege was older than Earth. He was a strong, but small, man. I could make out the outline of each of his muscles as he sat before the fire. He worked as hard as the younger men in the village did, if not harder. He preached that everyone must earn their keep and that a village is a family that works to take care of each other.

The elder motioned for me to sit on a woven blanket on the sand next to him, to his right. As I did, the Snype sat at my side, curling up next to me and looking for all the world like it was tucked down in a nest ready for a nap.

"I am pleased to see you and your Parent are well," Rege began. "Your brother was in good spirits also."

"I greatly apologize for any harm that my brother has done," I said lowering my head and looking off into the flames.

"There is nothing to apologize to us for, but he has left children who are not of Corton here."

His voice was soothing. I felt at ease as I sat in the presence of such a peaceful man. Everything about Corton was peaceful. It angered me to think of my brother disturbing a race that wished for nothing but harmony.

"Why did your brother bring those younglings here?" asked Rege.

"To anger me," I said.

I took a breath and looked at the Snype glowing next to me. He looked peaceful, lying next to the flames.

"They are the children of Earth," I continued. "He captured them because he is aware that they hold a place in my heart. I believe that he brought them to your home because he also knows how important Corton is to me."

"Well, whatever the circumstances, it is always a pleasure to be in the presence of angels," said Rege with a smile. "However, I would appreciate it if you could take the children back with you before more harm comes to the planet than your brother has already burdened us with. The energy he left behind is causing abnormalities in the behavior of the animals in the forest and the people of the village."

"I will take care of it right away," I assured him.

I had not taken into consideration how much energy Lucifer would have consumed from the planet in order to accomplish his goal of hiding the children there. I stood and went to where Rege sat. I knelt down at his side and leaned my forehead into his. He placed a hand on the back of my head and gently pressed my head against his. This was the respectful way to end a conversation and send a person on their way.

As I stood, the Snype stood and stretched its legs and neck. It shook, fluffing out its feathers. When it did, glittering flecks of light fell from the bird's body. He then began walking a few paces ahead of me once more, leading me to the lost children.

Soon, I was able to see a bright green glow on the edge of the horizon. I was getting close. He had led me in the right direction. It was in that moment that I knew that I was meant to save the children. I was meant to interfere with my own reaping and work to save the humans. She had not given up hope on them yet, so I needed to do everything in my power to fix what my brother and the humans had done.

I knew that the trumpets were still going to blow, the fate of the Earth was inevitable, but there was still hope. There was still Lumen, who I believed was the answer to saving Earth. I needed to get back to Melahem and pull him from the bitter grasp of Woodworm.

Once I was close enough to see the shadows of the children moving beneath Lucifer's dome, the trail stopped. The Snype turned to me sang one last melodic note before disappearing into the night, leaving Corton much like a released soul left Earth. It floated away, glistening though the night, its soul dancing among the stars, back into the heavens.

There was something different about the children. I could see their Lights through the thick energy dome that Lucifer had captured them in. I smiled at the ironic turn of the situation. In attempting to break me down, Lucifer captured and stole the lost children of Melahem, but in doing so he reopened their hearts. They were shining with the innocence that the city had stolen from them.

I could hear how shallow their breaths were. They were having difficulty breathing in the fresh Cortonian air. Each of them was wheezing and coughing, and I assumed it caused them pain to take in too much of the unpolluted air at once. They were used to the smog-filled atmosphere of Melahem.

As I stepped closer to the dome, each of the children took a step away from me in unison until they had retreated as far back in their prison cell as they could without touching its electric walls.

"I am not going to hurt you," I said. I was sure they believed me to be working with my brother. After all, we did look very similar in our appearance, from our pale white skin and solid black veins, lips and hair, to our attire, which was always black. Our eyes were over dilated and did not look human. I could see how anyone, not just a frightened child, would make the assumption.

"My name is Azrael," I said. "I am here to take you home."

My words did not seem to comfort the children. They still looked frightened. They could see me. They had their innocence; their Lights were glowing bright. That was enough. They would understand the rest in due time.

I took a step back and inspected the dome. It was strong. Lucifer had made the walls of energy thick and powerful. There was no way that I could break through Lucifer's barrier and still have enough energy to teleport all of the children and myself back to Melahem safely. I needed to be able to hold onto the children. If I lost my grasp on them, I would lose them in the great abyss of space.

I felt blessed that Lucifer had abandoned them on Corton, even if he was interfering with the lives of its inhabitants. The planet was filled with magic and energy. I pushed my hands deep in the rich soil. I closed my eyes for a moment and allowed the pure energy of the planet to course through me. It was invigorating. I could feel the strong connection between the plants and the animals and the people of the planet. They all coexisted in such harmony. It was an experience that humans had never been fully able to understand.

It was almost effortless for me to gather enough magic to engulf Lucifer's energy dome with my own. The energy on Corton was so strong and pure, I could protect myself from the electric shock of my brother's green electricity while still being able to hold onto the children.

I wondered if I would be able to use the energy of the planet to break down my brother's walls. I knew that I could seek assistance from the people of Corton, but they did not use magic in the same way as angels, so they would not be able to help me in breaking down the dome. The pure innocence of the planet affected the power that surged through it.

I also did not wish to disturb the planet's people any longer. The power that it would have taken to destroy the dome could have devastated the planet.

I grabbed hold of the blanket of energy that I coated the dome in and concentrated on the shambles of Melahem. I needed to get back to Lumen. I knew he would not be able to see me, but now that I had come to the realization that I could help him in ways that I had not realized, we would indeed be able to work to save the people of Melahem together.

As I concentrated, I could feel the molecules of my body begin to break apart. I was suspended in the air, along with the children, a large cloud of half-existence. I projected us through space. Although I could not see where I was going other than aiming at Melahem, I could feel as we passed planets and stars on our journey, weaving around comets and meteors with ease.

As we reached Melahem, the elements of my being merged back together. I had landed us just outside of the city, by the old oak tree that had shown me its memories. I turned to see the dome and all of the children reforming right in front me.

There were still battles to be fought, but for today, I knew I had accomplished something wonderful.

I watched as the little light that could make its way through the atmosphere faded away until I was left standing in the dark.

***

The sound of the fourth trumpet rang through the night.

THE SEVENTH TRUMPET
BOOK 2
LIFE IN THE SHADOWS

CHAPTER ONE

As the fourth trumpet sounded, the sky darkened. I could no longer see the faint hue of the moon breaking through the clouds. There were no longer any different shades of black and grey swirling above us. Sorrow washed over me as I realized that Melahem would no longer see any light that did not come from a flame; the planet would be left in darkness until the end.

As the shadows consumed the city, I heard an echoing sound in the distance that made my blood run cold: a deep howl from the direction of the desert. I recognized the sound from when I was sitting on the porch of the Waters' house the first time Lumen and I entered the desert together. It was not the howl of the wolf-like creatures we had encountered, but the howl of the beast I heard chasing them. The first was met with the voices of at least five more creatures howling in rounds, a choir of the night. As haunting as it was, it was also beautiful.

My mind raced as I thought about the beings encroaching on Melahem. With the natural light extinguished, those that ruled the night would be able to move freely whenever—and wherever—they pleased, no matter how far. They will have nothing to fear.

I stood with the children, silent, thinking about how I had just taken them from one planet filled with darkness to another. They were never going to be able to play in the sun again. I was going to have to work fast. I needed to release their souls before they felt the weight of humanity's mistakes crushing them into maturing, to facing reality, far too quickly for them to remain innocent.

I needed to break down the barrier of Lucifer's energy. I brought my hand up to the dome and let it hover just above the green shield. I could feel the heat coming off the barrier and I slowly moved my hand closer. I wanted to see if I could penetrate his energy just as I could walk through my own. I had not attempted the action on Corton in fear of not being able to get the children home, but now we were back on Melahem.

I took a deep breath and plunged my hand into the dome. I heard a few of the children scream in fear as I did so. A deep shock coursed through my arm. I could feel my body convulsing as the electricity surged through me. It felt as though my entire being was on fire. I worked to pull my arm from wall of the dome, but I could not gain enough control over my muscle movements to do so. I could barely control my breathing. I was stuck.

Panting, I forced my eyes closed. I held my arm as still as I could, focusing on my heartbeat. As I did, I was able to feel the path the energy was taking through my body, working its way through me in a circular motion.

I could feel when the energy was leaving my arm and traveling down to my leg, mapping out my figure. it was an odd sensation. As I concentrated, I was able to regain minimal control over my arm as the energy made its way out of my fingertips. Even with this slight control I did not have enough power to pull my arm free of the dome. Once my arm was clear of the electricity, I allowed my body to become stiff, and forced my weight backwards.

My mass pulled me back far enough that I was able to free most of my arm in the first try, but my hand was still caught at the wrist. I looked through the dome at its prisoners. They looked both fearful and amazed.

I focused on the children until I could feel the energy leaving my arm once more. I pushed all of my weight back, digging the heels of my boots into the dirt. My hand slipped free and I fell hard to the ground. I did not have enough control over my body to attempt to buffer the fall. I lay flat for a moment, waiting for the last few surges of electricity burning just beneath my skin to leave my body.

It felt like ages until I was able to regain control over my body and could rise, albeit shakily, to my feet. I needed to free the innocent as quickly as possible.

"Stand back," I instructed the children, and they huddled together in the back portion of the dome, crouching down as far away from where I was aiming as they could.

I pooled the little power I had left into one strong ball. Bright colors swirled as I pushed my energy into Lucifer's. The dome absorbed everything I threw at it. My purple and white light mixed with Lucifer's green. I signed, realizing that I had not penetrated the power source; in fact, I might have reinforced it.

I dropped to the ground in frustration. I was not going to allow myself to be defeated this easily, but I was not strong enough to summon any more energy. I was not sure I was going to be able to stand back up on my own. I needed help.

I needed Lumen.

***

About the Author

Crystal Clark is an emerging writer from southeast Michigan. She has been writing and drawing up stories ever since she can remember. She read her first completed story—that she wrote and illustrated—to her class in the second grade. Writing has always been a release and a coping mechanism for her.

Her first chapbook of poetry, *From Frost to Phoenix*, was published by The Poet's Haven and her poem *One* has been nominated for the Pushcart Poetry Prize.

Crystal holds a Bachelor's degree in Psychology from Central Michigan University and a Master's degree in Applied Behavior Analysis from Kaplan University.

To learn more about Crystal, visit:

https://www.facebook.com/The-Seventh-Trumpet-108508260735226/
https://crystalclarkwritting.blogspot.com/
https://www.instagram.com/theseventhtrumpetseries/?hl=en

ALL THINGS THAT MATTER PRESS

FOR MORE INFORMATION ON TITLES AVAILABLE FROM
ALL THINGS THAT MATTER PRESS, GO TO
http://allthingsthatmatterpress.com

www.ingramcontent.com/pod-product-compliance
Lightning Source LLC
Chambersburg PA
CBHW072009170626
46813CB00005B/2081